STILLWATER TIDES

STEENA HOLMES

WELCOME TO STILLWATER BAY

STEENA HOLMES

www.steenaholmes.com
www.facebook.com/steenaholmes.author
www.twitter.com/steenaholmes

Any similarities found between my fictional event and town and anything found on the news is purely coincidental.

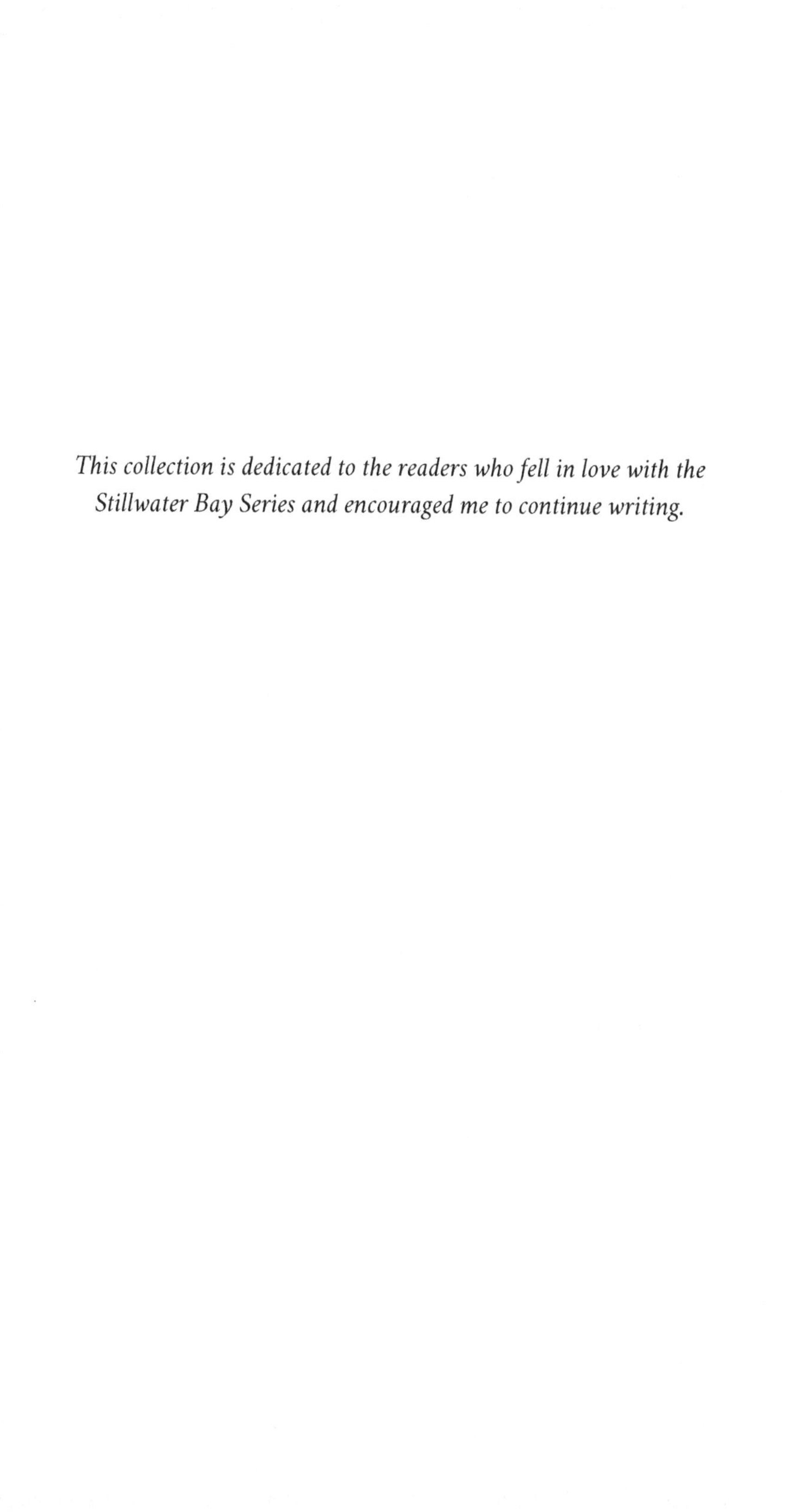

This collection is dedicated to the readers who fell in love with the Stillwater Bay Series and encouraged me to continue writing.

STILLWATER BAY MAP

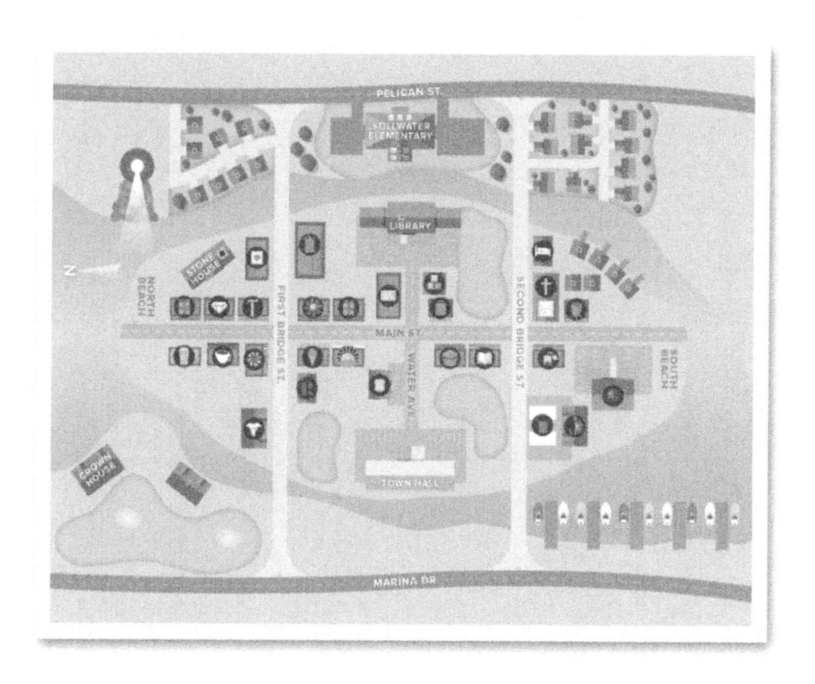

LETTER FROM STEENA

Thank you for joining with me on a this journey. The community of Stillwater has become very dear to my heart and I hope you will feel the same way. In my fictional town of Stillwater Bay a tragedy hits that affects every single member of the community. The series is not meant to focus on the event, but rather the aftermath, or the healing.

In this series are the following stories:

Stillwater Shores

Stillwater Rising

Stillwater Tides

Stillwater Deep

Steena Holmes

STILLWATER

A Stillwater Bay Series

TIDES

STEENA HOLMES

NEW YORK TIMES BESTSELLING AUTHOR

STILLWATER TIDES

STILLWATER BAY SERIES

STEENA HOLMES

www.steenaholmes.com
www.facebook.com/steenaholmes.author
www.twitter.com/steenaholmes

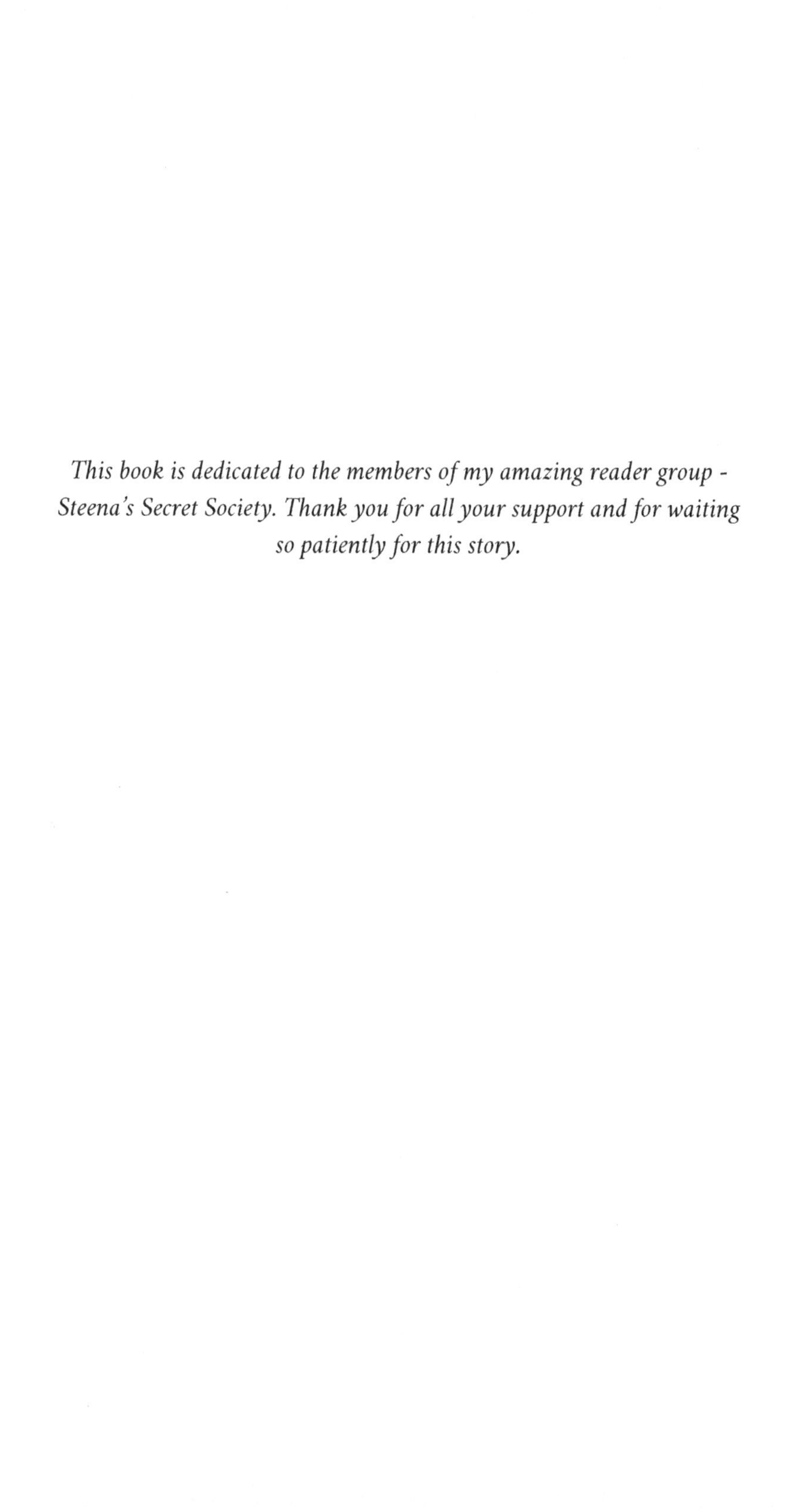

This book is dedicated to the members of my amazing reader group - Steena's Secret Society. Thank you for all your support and for waiting so patiently for this story.

ISBN: 978-1-987877-08-3

ISBN: 978-0-9920555-5-4

DEAR READERS

Sometimes we will read stories that touch our hearts and won't let go...so many of you have told me that my Stillwater Bay series is like that. If that's why you picked up Stillwater Tides - thank you!

It's because of readers like *you* that I was able to write this story.

I hope you will enjoy this little look into Stillwater Bay and the community there. I love writing about the community members of this town and how they rise above the tragedy that hit their town. I hope you will too.

Happy Reading

Steena Holmes

1

GRACE

Babies shouldn't cry like this.

They should be filled with life and laughter, and eyes round with wonder and delight.

They should feel peace, safe and wanted. Loved.

They shouldn't cry as if their hearts broke over and over and over with every breath that entered their tiny bodies.

They should never cry this hard.

"Shh, little one, shhh." Grace rubbed Sophie's back, bouncing her gently in her arms while walking in circles in an attempt to calm her. Gas in the infant's tummy bubbled beneath her hand and she sighed with frustration.

No wonder you're unhappy.

"Shhh, it's all going to be okay. Your daddy should be home soon." Grace's voice remained low and steady.

Between the diaper rash she'd discovered this morning and now the gas, Grace didn't blame Sophie for her tears. She'd been shocked this morning when she changed the girl's diaper. Her little behind and the backs of her legs were bright red, with a few raised welts.

"Your father should know better," Grace muttered.

While bouncing the baby in her arms, Grace took out her phone to hit the voice-record button, something she did often to leave herself notes. Nathan needed help and if anyone could help, it was Lacie. She ran the local moms-and-tots groups in town.

She thought about how soaked Sophie had been when he'd handed her over this morning and sighed. "I don't think your daddy has read any of those parenting magazines or articles I've left lying around for him, has he?" She kissed the top of Sophie's head and breathed in that fresh baby-wash smell. "If he had, he would know by now that you need your diaper changed more often."

She worked hard to keep the frustration out of her voice. The last thing little Sophie needed was to have more negativity in her life.

Gradually Sophie quietened and Grace breathed a sigh of relief as the baby fell asleep. In the room she'd converted into a nursery, Grace hit the play button on the iPod sitting on the dresser and waited for the sounds of soft classical music to fill the room. Sophie snuggled in close, and Grace wasn't quite ready to relinquish her hold, especially since she wasn't crying anymore, so she sat down in the corner rocker and closed her eyes, letting the music wash over her as she rocked gently.

Memories of a time she would rather forget haunted her as the emotion within the music struck a chord.

Breaking news. There have been reports of gunfire from a small town on the coast of Washington. Eyewitnesses are claiming that a young man has opened fire within the walls of Stillwater Elementary School....

Her heart pounding, Grace opened her eyes and forced the memory of the radio announcer's stunned voice to silence.

Not comforting silence.

Deadly silence.

Sophie fussed, as if recognizing Grace's stress, so she breathed in deep, filling her lungs up until they hurt before releasing the air slowly and steadily.

With Sophie finally asleep, Grace placed her in the crib and stared at her angelic face. She'd never seen a more beautiful baby. When she wasn't crying, there was a peacefulness on Sophie's face that eased an ache in Grace's heart.

To keep the memories at bay, she needed to be busy. She'd planned on tacking her garden and with Sophie asleep, there was no time like the present.

Her poor roses and other plants were smothered by weeds or dying due to lack of water. In some sections she didn't even know which was which—weed or flower. She knew she should have kept the markers with the names of the plants in the places she'd planted each one, as John had suggested. She thought she'd remember. She thought wrong. She forgot a lot of things lately.

Although it wasn't so much forgetting as not caring. She had other things to focus on. Other things to worry about. Whether or not she planted irises beside orchids or whatever was out there wasn't really a priority. Not right now.

But it wouldn't hurt to try. So she spent the next hour working in one small section, pulling what she hoped were weeds and not plants before giving up. It was time to face the fact: She was not a gardener. Not like Katie had been.

Thinking of her best friend hurt. It physically hurt. Her throat swelled and ached from struggling to swallow, and her eyes burned, as if she'd stared into the sun for too long.

Grace rubbed her dirty hands over her shorts before she could stop herself and her breath hitched at the stains she left behind.

Blood.

It looked like blood. Blood she'd wiped without thought to clean her hands before reaching out to one of her students.

Blood that coated her skin when she'd knelt beside Katie in their kindergarten classroom at the school after fighting her way through the crowds and emergency personnel to ensure her students and fellow teacher were safe.

Grace stared at her hand and shivered, her hands shaking at the memory. Flashes of Katie's face, the sounds of the screams and sirens in the background as Grace rushed to the side of the school where her kindergarten classroom was located hit her hard, and she couldn't breathe.

Her lungs constricted and a wave of pain tore through her chest, forcing Grace to lie down on the ground, her back pressed hard against the grass while she stared blankly up at the clouds, compelling her body to relax, her lungs to let in the air she needed.... She tried to calm her body, to get through this panic attack.

Her therapist had warned they would hit her like this.

It took several minutes, but eventually she grounded herself and was able to sit up and not feel like her lungs were about to shrivel to the size of raisins.

She hated those memories. Hated how they came out of nowhere, how almost everything she did was tethered back to a memory of that day.

She needed to think about something else. Anything else.

One thing her therapist had said was to reach out as often and as much as she needed whenever the memories of that day surfaced.

There were only three people she normally would have wanted to talk to.

John. But lately conversations between her and her husband had been...awkward.

Faith. But Grace wasn't quite ready to face her sister. Not yet.

And Katie.

But her best friend was dead.

So instead she called Paige.

"One word," Grace said as soon as Paige answered her phone. "Garden."

"So you're finally going to take me up on my offer to help?" Paige Bloomin's voice held a hint of laughter, but mainly Grace heard exhaustion and sadness.

"Yes and yes. If you have time."

"For you? I'll make time," Paige said.

Grace groaned and hit the speaker button on her phone before she sat down on a lawn chair. "You're busy, aren't you?"

Paige snorted. "Things are a little crazy, but it's all good."

Grace frowned. She wondered how much of that craziness had to do with Paige attempting to distract herself from what happened in their small town.

Two months had passed since the school shooting, but the effects still lingered. There wasn't a single person in Stillwater Bay who hadn't been affected by the events of that day. Paige had lost someone special, someone she'd thought about having a future with. Someone who happened to be in the wrong place at the wrong time, just like Katie.

Neither one should have died.

No one should have.

"Do you remember what plants you had and where you planted them?"

"You're kidding me, right?" While she'd always wished she had a green thumb, Grace had to accept that when it came to gardening, her thumb was indeed quite black.

Paige's sigh was loud enough for Grace's neighbors to hear. "What happened to the notebook I gave you to keep all the info in? We even sketched out the garden and where you wanted plants."

"Honestly, I'm sure it's here somewhere. I just have no idea where." Nor was she really inclined to look.

"I'll pop over tonight. How much of it is still alive?"

Grace looked over her garden. Other than her rosebushes and a few shrubs, she had no idea.

"I'll take your silence as almost none?" Paige said.

"The roses are okay, I think. There're buds on them, at least. I had to clip a few blooms off because they looked like they'd been half-eaten by something."

Paige didn't reply, but Grace knew she was rolling her eyes at her. She just knew it.

"I have a few clients to deal with today; then I'd planned to stop at Katie's and take a look at her garden. No doubt Nathan doesn't have time for it, and she—"

"Always was proud of her flowers," Grace whispered.

"Right." Paige cleared her throat. "I need to stop by the shop too for a bit, so..." Her voice trailed off, but Grace could read between the lines.

"Why don't you come by for dinner? Look over the garden, we'll share a bottle of wine, and then you can come back tomorrow or whenever to fix my disaster?" she suggested.

"That's a great idea." The relief in Paige's voice was noticeable. "I'll see you later."

Grace leaned back in the chair, her face raised to the sun, and closed her eyes. She should probably tell John that Paige was coming over and then think about what to make.

Her hand hovered over her phone before she dropped it. She didn't really need to call and tell him; she could just wait till he was home and casually mention it.

It actually would be a nice change to have someone else sit at the table with them, someone to help keep the conversation flowing, rather than the stilted silence that seemed to grow between them with each passing day.

Grace knew they weren't the only couple who were struggling since the tragedy, but they probably were the only ones refusing to see a counselor for it.

Grace didn't see a reason to go. John did. He wanted to work on their marriage, but in order to do that, Grace knew she'd have to work through...whatever she was going through. And she didn't want to.

It didn't mean John had stopped trying, though. Case in point, her cell phone buzzed with a message from the man himself.

Heading home. Forgot a report I printed off last night. I've got coffee.

Grace's breath caught.

Which report? I'll have it ready for you.

She could meet him at the door and then wave good-bye as he drove off. No need for him to come into the house, and especially no need to stay.

Except he never replied.

Frantic now, Grace headed back inside and washed her hands, being sure to scrub the dirt from beneath her nails before she searched his office and found the report she thought he needed.

She was sitting out on the front porch swing, leg bouncing nervously by the time he pulled up.

It was hard not to smile instinctively as John raised the coffees he'd brought and winked.

Those little butterflies that announced the quickening of love fluttered, and not for the first time Grace wished she could rewind time back to when things were simpler and they were very much in love.

Once upon a time when John would come home early, they'd head straight to the bedroom, forgetting about the coffees until they were cold.

Now...her fingers tightened around the report she held and she struggled to find words to mask her nervousness.

He sat beside her on the swing, close enough for their legs to touch.

"I grabbed that report for you." She handed him the file without looking at him.

"Thanks. I'd made some notes on it last night that I forgot to enter in the document." He took the file, leaving it beside him. "Did you get any gardening done?"

She laughed briefly. "Enough to know I need Paige to do the

rest. She's coming for dinner, by the way." She sneaked a look over at him.

He nodded and glanced up at the hanging pots on their porch. "Think she could fix those too?"

Grace wrinkled her nose. "I'll just buy new planters for that. And I'll try to remember to water them." She took a sip of her latte and sighed with satisfaction. Gina, the owner of a little café named after herself, made the best in town. "Thanks for the coffee."

Their conversation was stilted, mundane, and skirted across anything remotely personal. Much as their entire relationship seemed to go lately.

She was surprised when he leaned over and placed a gentle kiss on her cheek. "Anything for you."

She searched his gaze, read more than she wanted to behind the love and acceptance she saw, and looked toward the front door with hesitation.

John followed her gaze. "Am I keeping you from something?"

She shook her head, sipping her coffee to keep from saying anything.

"I should be home early." He touched her knee, squeezing lightly. "Maybe I can help you with dinner?"

She nodded. "You can barbecue while I make a pasta salad and —" A car pulled up to the curb.

Grace felt like swearing, something she rarely did.

John's hand left her knee, tightening into a fist before relaxing.

She'd purposely asked Nathan to come early, but it was barely after noon.

"Expecting company?" There was an edge to her husband's voice that didn't surprise Grace at all.

She sighed, rubbing her forehead, but didn't say anything. It wouldn't have mattered regardless.

"Guess I should have given you more notice I was coming

home." The sarcasm in John's voice was thick as his lips thinned and a muscle in his cheek pulsed.

"It's not like that and you know it," Grace said beneath her breath as Nathan approached.

"Really?" John stood and moved away from her, leaning on the railing of their porch, arms crossed as he stared at the man who stood there with an awkward smile on his face.

"Hey, guys." Nathan Hansen stuck his hands in his jeans pockets.

"You're early." Grace attempted to smile despite the obvious tension.

"Really?" Nathan looked distressed. He glanced at his watch and winced. "Sorry."

"Don't apologize. It's not like I gave you a time or anything." Grace attempted to keep her tone light, not missing the obvious look of relief on Nathan's face.

"Aren't you supposed to be working or something?" John asked.

Nathan shrugged. "I've got quite the backup of assignments to tackle, but Arnold has been good, given my situation."

"Situation," John muttered. There was a look on his face she couldn't read. "We've all got situations, man."

Nathan blanched, his hand reaching for the ledge of the balcony. "I know, sorry, it's just…I meant—"

"It's okay, Nathan. We understand," Grace quickly interjected.

"Sure we do, buddy." John's words were laced with sarcasm. "Just like we understood the past times you've used what happened to you as an excuse to use my wife. Because that's what you're doing, right?" He shook his head and pushed to his feet.

"John," Grace said softly.

"Thanks for the file. Guess I know now why you met me out here and not inside." His lips tightened into a grimace. "I'll see you when I get back home."

Grace looked at her husband, tried to tell him how she felt

through her gaze, but he either wasn't listening or didn't want to know.

She was sorry, she wanted to say.

It's not what you think, she tried to say.

You don't understand, she needed to say.

But she didn't say anything, and only watched as he eventually drove off.

She turned to the reason Nathan was here—for his daughter. "Sophie's asleep."

"I'm sorry." Nathan leaned against the rail, his legs crossed, his shoulders hunched.

Grace shook her head. "There's nothing for you to apologize about."

"I hate to wake her." He looked down the street. "Maybe I should take her home, though. I can… I'll call my mom and see if she can watch her. It's not fair to you…." He shuffled his feet.

Grace sat up straight. "No."

She'd made a promise to Katie that if anything should ever happen to her, Grace would always be there to watch over Sophie, to help raise her.

It was the least she could do.

"Nathan, it's fine. Trust me. Besides, I already promised you I'd take care of Sophie for the summer while you're at work. It's no trouble, believe me."

"You're sure?" The hopefulness in his voice eased her heart.

"I'm positive. Head on home and I'll walk her over when she wakes up, okay?"

He nodded and turned to leave. "Actually, I'll probably just go back to the office then, if you don't mind." Nathan worked as an editor for the *Stillwater News,* and also helped to maintain the Whidbey Island tourism Web site and community magazine. "Bring her there maybe? I have a couple more calls I was putting off that I could make, and I'm sure the girls at work would love to see her. They keep begging me to bring her by."

"Absolutely. It's a nice day for a walk, and the motion of the stroller seems to soothe her," Grace said, hoping her tone wasn't too pointed. Nathan had to learn these things about his daughter.

Nathan nodded and looked away. "I'm going to start working from home soon."

She nodded. He'd said that almost weekly to her. One day he'd mean it.

"You should probably start sooner, rather than later. You look exhausted, Nathan." There were dark circles beneath his eyes, his jaw was covered in a scruff she knew Katie would never have tolerated, and his shoulders slumped, making him look almost bowed over. "You can't keep doing this to yourself—or to Sophie."

"I know."

Grace sighed. "I picked up a new parenting book; it might give you some suggestions. I started to look through it last night, and I'll add Post-It notes to the pages you should look at."

"Thanks. I appreciate it." He half turned to leave, then stopped. "I really do, Grace. I don't know how I would do this without you." He swallowed hard, and a haunted look crept into his eyes. "I know Katie..."

The sound of her best friend's name punched into her heart, bruising her in a way she'd never heal from. "Katie would have done the same." She blinked rapidly to dispel the tears that threatened, even now, to gather. "It'll get easier soon. It has to." She attempted a brief smile but knew he didn't believe her.

She didn't even believe herself.

"Have you taken her out for a walk at all, Nathan?" she asked him. "I find it always helps calm her. You might want to try it when you can't get her to sleep at night."

He shook his head. "It seems like so much work, getting her ready, making sure I have everything, and what if..." He stopped and shrugged. "I know, I know. I should. Maybe tonight I will."

It was the same thing she'd heard over and over from him.

John said Nathan used her as his crutch when it came to his daughter, and at times she agreed with him.

But it wasn't fair that Nathan was now a single father to a baby and forced to raise Sophie on his own, and Grace needed to make it up to him somehow.

To make it up to Katie.

To make it up to her own baby. The one she lost shortly after the shooting.

She could never atone for what had happened, but she could try to make it right. Make Nathan's life easier.

"Nathan, you need to find ways that work for you to calm her. She needs you," she said softly.

A stricken look filled his eyes. "This was all Katie's area, you know? She was the one who read all the books and parenting magazines and would know exactly what to do. God," he groaned, "Sophie was supposed to be raised by two parents, not just one."

Guilt, the weight of it heavier than she could carry already, almost drowned her with his words. The shame, the grief, but most of all, the guilt of what happened that day threatened to crush her.

"I know," she said. "I'm so sorry."

***

For the next hour as Sophie slept, Grace cleaned her house with a manic passion. She'd sent John a text attempting to break the tension between them, but he'd yet to respond.

Not that she blamed him.

Hopefully he'd come home before Paige arrived and they could talk. He hated that she was taking care of Sophie, and Grace hated that and whatever friendship had been between him and Nathan had all but dissipated over the past few months.

They used to be inseparable, the four of them—Katie and Nathan, her and John. Best friends, always together, doing couple things...she and Katie used to chuckle about growing old together and getting side-by-side suites at the local retirement home.

Until *the* day Grace called Katie asking her to cover her morning class. When she decided to play hooky and leave early to see her sister in Seattle. When Katie ended up being the one to protect the lives of their kindergarten students with her own body while Grace drove down the highway, window down and music turned up.

The day everything changed.

Grace peeked into the room where Sophie slept and was surprised to find the little one lying there, wide-awake and with a smile on her face. "Well, hello, there."

Sophie's arms reached out the moment Grace appeared at her side.

"Look who's awake and happy." Grace picked her up and snuggled the four-month-old close to her chest, gently kissing her on the top of her head. She loved this baby more than she thought possible.

As she repacked Sophie's bag and prepared for their daily walk, she noticed a magazine she'd set to the side that was flipped open. It was all on bonding with your baby, and she stuffed it into the bag. Hopefully Nathan would read it.

Sophie loved the walks. Grace thought it must be the vibration of the pavement beneath the wheels that helped soothe her, because she never cried while in the stroller.

She made her way down Second Bridge Street, taking her time as she walked along the bridge. The water was calm but crowded with motorboats heading out into the bay. She waved to those below and then caught sight of Charlotte Stone up ahead—Grace usually ran into the mayor on her walks, often stopping to say hello.

She'd been so impressed with Charlotte and her husband

Jordan, the principal of Stillwater Elementary. Without those two as a team, she really wasn't sure how the town would have managed to survive. Every day they'd been there for the families affected by the shooting, worked with the hordes of reporters that swarmed the town, and somehow kept their calm.

They were heroes to many in their community—Grace included.

"It's a beautiful day for a walk, isn't it?" Charlotte greeted her as Grace swerved off the sidewalk and onto a path that went through a small park.

"We've had great weather this summer so far."

"I thought you were planning on gardening today?" Charlotte smiled down into the stroller and let Sophie grab hold of one of her fingers.

"I did, or rather, I tried." She shrugged. "I can't seem to keep things alive around me." The smile that was on her face disappeared and her stomach dropped as she realized what she'd just said. She knew from her sad smile that Charlotte caught her words.

"With plants," Grace clarified. She swallowed hard.

"You should call Paige for help."

Grace nodded. "It's like you read my mind. She's coming over for dinner tonight."

"If anyone can fix your flowers, it's her. She's a natural." Charlotte smiled. "Headed anywhere special today or just out for a walk?"

"I'm taking Sophie here to see her daddy." Grace smiled down at Sophie, who was stuffing her fist in her mouth. "What about you? Where are you headed?"

"Just my daily walk." Charlotte glanced around. "I don't like to spend much time in my office during the summer if I can help it." Charlotte's smile didn't reach her eyes. "We've missed having you take part in the teddy-bear picnics." She glanced down at Sophie.

"I know." Grace looked away, feeling a stab of guilt. "I just never know how Sophie will be, and I figured you probably have more than enough help."

A slight frown marred Charlotte's face. "No one could replace you. Have you thought more about my offer to find some teenagers willing to babysit Sophie during the day?"

Grace shook her head. "I love being with Sophie."

Charlotte gave her a penetrating stare.

"I feel closer to Katie when I'm holding her daughter," Grace admitted. She moved the stroller back and forth once Sophie started to fuss in an attempt to ease her. She appreciated the distraction. It was nice of Charlotte to care, to be concerned for her, but she didn't need to be.

"I understand," Charlotte said quietly. "I'm here if you need me; you know that, right?"

Grace nodded. Everyone in town knew that. Sometimes she wondered who was there for Charlotte, but just as quickly she pushed the idea from her mind. Charlotte was surrounded by amazing friends, a strong group within the community. She wasn't alone.

Besides, she had Jordan to lean on. If anything they'd proved to be stronger because of the tragedy that hit their town. Nothing could tear them apart.

"Enjoy the rest of your walk, Grace." Charlotte gently squeezed her forearm.

Grace took in a deep breath and held it for a few seconds, letting it fill her before she released it and continued on her walk.

Filling the hole in her heart...nothing could do that.

Shortly after losing her best friend in the school shooting, Grace had suffered a miscarriage. She lost her own child, the child she'd dreamed about for years.

People thought it was easy to move past a miscarriage, but what they didn't realize was that it was still a death to be grieved. A death of dreams, of wishes and hopes for a future.

She glanced down to find Sophie staring up at her with wide eyes.

"And what are you staring at, Sophie mine? Is that a smile I see? You like our walks, don't you?" Katie used to talk to her daughter all the time, even while she was pregnant. She'd play music all the time as well—probably one of the reasons Sophie calmed and slept so peacefully at Grace's home with the iPod playing.

There was a sharp pain in her chest that Grace rubbed away while she continued on her walk.

Camille Bloomin, Paige's older sister, was arranging flowers in the buckets outside her shop. Grace noticed a bundle of wildflowers and was immediately drawn to them. Katie loved wildflowers and would fill her house with them whenever she could. They used to go out and pick them together on weekends.

"They're beautiful, aren't they? I just received a fresh load." Camille picked out a bouquet and held it out, the flowers vibrant in lavender, soft blue, and bright pink.

"I'll take two, please," Grace said. She pulled out some money from her wallet and handed it to Camille, who headed inside her store. Grace was going to follow, but when she noticed the boxes of flowers all over the floor inside, she stayed where she was. There was no way she could maneuver the stroller in there.

"You should tell your husband I'm having a sale this weekend. It's been a while since he's come in, and you shouldn't be buying flowers for yourself." Camille placed the bouquets in a brown bag for her and handed her the change.

Flowers were the last things John would buy her right now.

"I think he's trying to make a subtle point with me. We spent a lot of money on potted plants for the porch and backyard and I kind of let them all die." Her nose wrinkled at the admission, and she wasn't surprised to see the mirth in Camille's eyes.

"Didn't that happen last year too?"

Grace nodded. "And the year before that as well." She

shrugged. “I like the idea of plants and flowers, but…they don’t seem to like me all that much.”

Camille’s brows rose. “You do know we can help you with that, right?”

“I do. I sweet-talked Paige into coming over for dinner tonight in hopes she’ll take a look at my disastrous garden and attempt to fix it. I might as well put you guys on retainer. You’re more than welcome to join us too, if you’d like?”

Camille bent down and rearranged the flowers in the bucket at her feet. “Thanks for the invite, but all I want to do tonight is relax in my tub with a glass of wine and a good book.” She looked down the street toward the corner. “How’s the little one doing?” She turned her head to smile at Sophie, her facial features softening.

“A bit overtired, but that seems to be normal lately. One day she’ll figure out she needs to sleep.”

“How’s Nathan? Last time I saw him he appeared a bit haggard.”

Grace swallowed. She didn’t feel comfortable talking about Nathan or how he was handling his grief. That was his story to tell, not hers.

“He’s okay.” She pushed the stroller forward a smidgen. “We’re actually on our way to see him right now.” She stopped herself from saying anything more. Why did she continually feel the need to explain herself or him or why she was always taking care of his daughter? It was no one’s business but their own.

After saying good-bye, she continued down the street toward Water Avenue, which crossed Main Street. On one end were the library and newspaper office, and on the other were the town hall and the new memorial that had just been set up.

No matter how many times she saw the memorial, she found she couldn’t breathe for a few moments.

The large silica-glass heart molded from sand struck by lightning shone as the sun hit it, but what really stood out was the smaller glass heart within etched with the names of those who lost their lives in the May school shooting.

It was beautiful and breathtakingly heart-wrenching at the same time. Battery-lit candles and bouquet of flowers encircled the statue, and as usual, tears welled up in Grace's eyes at the outpouring of love the town had shown.

Every time she saw the memorial, the knowledge that her name should have been etched on that glass instead of Katie's hit her hard.

She added her own small bouquet of wildflowers to the others, her fingers reaching out to touch Katie's name.

"It should have been me," she whispered.

"I don't think she would agree with you."

Grace blushed at being heard and turned to see the reporter who remained in town standing slightly behind her.

"Grace, is it? I'm Samantha." She reached out her hand. "I don't think we've ever been formally introduced."

Grace cautiously shook her hand, wishing she were anywhere but here. She'd done her best to avoid Samantha, even to the point of turning the other way each time she saw her walking down the sidewalk.

Samantha nodded. "And this must be little Sophie. Her dad talks about her all the time when he's in the office."

Grace's brows knitted together. How did she know Nathan?

"I'm doing some freelance work for the *Stillwater News* for the summer."

"I thought you would have returned home for another assignment by now?" Grace pretended to be interested.

"I decided to take a little vacation."

Grace's brows rose. "In Stillwater? After all that happened?"

"I fell in love with this town, with the people. There's something here that... Actually, I'd love to talk to you, if I could. I'm working on some articles about the people here in Stillwater." Samantha stood there, her hands relaxed at her sides, and smiled.

Grace didn't smile back. She frowned and thought about how to take her leave. The last thing she wanted was to talk to a reporter.

"Arnold gave me your name."

Grace groaned. "There are days I hate that man, and it's not just because he's my husband's boss," she mumbled beneath her breath.

Samantha laughed. "I've yet to meet an editor I like." She sobered at her words, but a mask quickly came down over her face. It was amazing the immediate change.

There was a story there; Grace was sure of it.

Samantha fished a business card from her purse and held it out. "How about we meet for coffee at Gina's one day this week when you have time?"

It took everything in her not to rebuff the woman immediately. Talk to a reporter? About the people of Stillwater? After all the articles already written about them? After all the laundry airing and privacy stealing by the reporters that flooded their town for months following the school shooting?

"When I have time," Grace said. She pocketed the card. She'd talk to Nathan before she spoke to Samantha, find out what the woman wanted. Maybe he could talk to her instead.

She wasn't sure what else Samantha hoped to glean over a coffee. By now the whole world knew more details about the teenage shooter, Gabriel Berry, than necessary. Their principal had been made into the town hero, and Charlotte, the mayor, was apparently the glue to keeping this town from falling apart.

She wasn't sure what else Samantha wanted to learn. Unless it was about Katie.

Grace knew there was one significant detail that had been glossed over in all the papers.

2

CAMILLE

Camille leaned back from the floral arrangement she was working on and stretched her lower back, digging the knuckles on her fist into a tight knot that wouldn't go away.

What she needed was a massage, but she didn't have time for one, not to mention the money. Whatever she'd been able to put away needed to go to Paige. As hard as her sister tried to hide it, Camille knew her knee was causing her pain.

Stubborn brat.

"Who are you talking to?" Anne Marie, her friend and owner of Sweet Bakes, popped her head into Still Bloomin.

Camille's head jerked up and her cheeks flushed with embarrassment before she broke into a smile.

"Depends on what it was you heard." Luckily it was only Anne Marie who heard her. It could have been worse.

"The only person you call a stubborn brat is your sister, but you seem to be alone, so..." Anne Marie's lips quirked into a smile before she stepped in and pushed a box out of the way with her foot. "Do you need help?"

Camille tightened her lips for a split second. "I told Paige we were getting a delivery today and that I needed her this morning." She glanced at her watch. "It's now afternoon and she still hasn't shown up."

"Ahh." Anne Marie nodded before she knelt and started to open a box. "I've got some time; what can I do to help?"

Camille stretched the muscles in her back and groaned at the popping noises along her spine. "Sit with me for a bit. I could use the break. My feet are killing me."

Camille caught her friend's glance toward the shoes she wore and she blushed. "I know, I know. Not very smart." She sat on a stool and attempted to hide her feet as best she could.

She'd found an old pair of flats that she thought she'd lost this morning and couldn't resist. She loved these shoes. They were bright pink and sparkled whenever light hit them, and there was a cute little bow at the top...but they weren't meant to be worn for long periods. They were more for dress-up—as in dressing up for those dates she never had anymore.

"You should keep a spare pair of comfy shoes with you, maybe hidden beneath the counter or in the back. It's what I do. Nothing beats flip-flops for those hot summer days, or my orthotics that could double as slippers." Anne Marie set her purse on the counter before sitting down. She reached inside and pulled out a brown paper bag that had Camille's stomach growling.

The air filled with the subtle aroma of vanilla as Anne Marie opened the bag opened and pulled out two scones each the size of a fist. "Vanilla-bean scones, as requested."

"I didn't mean you had to make them. If I remember correctly, last night I asked for a recipe." Camille relaxed her shoulders and took the offered scone. She watched as her friend also brought out two plastic knives and a small jar of homemade strawberry jam.

"The last time you attempted a recipe of mine you made hockey pucks."

"Is it my fault I mistook baking soda for powder?" Camille rolled her eyes before she cut her scone in half and slathered it with the jam. She moaned with delight as she took a bite, and the two sat in silence while they devoured the baked treats.

"I was going to ask you to join me for lunch at Gina's, but if you're alone, I doubt you have time." Anne Marie wiped her mouth with a napkin and looked around her. "What about one of your summer students? Couldn't you get them to come in and help?"

Camille shook her head. "They're manning the booth down at the beach. Plus, this is something Paige and I take care of. She's the one who should be helping me."

"Where is she?"

Camille got up and knelt at one of the boxes on the floor. She began to sort through a variety of vases and small ornaments meant to go into various floral arrangements.

"Great question. She's either tending to one of our clients' gardens or possibly at the golf course." She looked at her watch. "I'm going with golf course, although she should have been done by now."

"The golf course? Is she there every day?"

"Yes. She doesn't need to be and she knows that. But..."

"She feels a connection to Ethan there, doesn't she?"

"She does. I never realized things were that serious between them. I mean, they never even went on a date."

Ethan Poole, the clubhouse manager at the Stillwater Golf Course, had been one of the victims of the school shooting in May. He'd been there to drop off his nephew's backpack that'd been left in his pickup truck and unfortunately ended up being at the wrong place at the wrong time. The day of the shooting, Paige admitted that Ethan had asked her on a date, and Camille had known from Paige's reaction that her sister liked him. But she hadn't realized just how much.

"How is his family doing?"

Camille shook her head. "I'm not sure. Paige would be the one to ask. She keeps in touch with Nick, his brother, but she doesn't really say much to me about anything."

The look Anne Marie gave her was assessing.

"What?" Camille asked. Her friend had a way of seeing straight into her soul sometimes. "Does it bother me that she keeps things from me? Yes, but what can I do?" It more than bothered her. It scared her. Her sister had slowly been withdrawing, and Camille was at a loss as to how to fix things between them.

"Things haven't gotten better, then?"

"Between us, you mean? No." She emptied the box of bubble-wrapped packages, then took the empty box and set it behind the counter with a bunch of others that needed to be broken down and put in the recycling bin behind their store.

"What are you doing for dinner tonight?"

Caught off guard by the question, Camille scratched the back of her neck. "Nothing really."

"Let's do dinner at Gina's. I won't take no for an answer."

"Then I won't say it. I'd love to." She smiled at her friend before filling her arms with the packages she'd placed on the floor. "Now, before you leave, check out these little figurines I ordered. They'll be perfect for the beach booth, I think."

While they carefully unwrapped each tiny piece, Paige walked in through the back door, a coffee tray in hand.

"Look who showed up." Camille tried really hard to keep the sarcasm out of her voice.

"I've been tending clients' gardens; you knew that." Paige's brow furrowed before she set the tray down. "Anne Marie, I picked up coffee for you too. I was going to bring it over and sweet-talk you into—"

"A scone? There's one in here for you." Anne Marie pushed the brown bag forward while Paige's eyes lit up. She chuckled as Paige reached in for a scone and groaned as she brought it up to her nose and inhaled. "You're just like your sister."

"If I haven't said it before, I love you."

"Funny how you usually tell me that when there's baking involved." Anne Marie gestured to the jam. "It's the batch you helped me make last month. Turned out pretty well."

"Awesome. I haven't opened my jars yet, so that's good to know." Paige sat down on the stool Camille had vacated and enjoyed her scone.

Camille continued to unwrap the figurines, being sure to smooth out the bubble wrap so they could use it later, and didn't say a word.

Anne Marie must have caught the tension between the two sisters, since she gathered her purse and coffee and stood. "I'll see you at closing."

Camille sighed and walked to the door. "Thanks for the scones," she said.

"No problem. I've got a container of extras for you for later too." She reached out and gently touched Camille's arm. "Be gentle with her."

Camille nodded but didn't say anything. She'd caught the way Paige tried to hide her limp earlier as she walked in.

She'd waved to a few people as they passed by, rearranged one of the flower buckets, and moved the sign she kept outside before she felt more in control of her emotions.

"These turned out to be really cute." Paige held up one of the figurines as soon as Camille walked back into the shop. They were sand dollars and seashells on sticks for flower bouquets. "I'm glad we ordered them."

Camille nodded. It was the only thing she trusted herself to do. If she opened her mouth, who knew what she'd say? So instead she kept her focus on peeling back the bubble wrap, careful not to pop too many of the bubbles.

"I'm sorry I wasn't here earlier." Paige kicked her feet along the floor, a guilty look on her face.

"I told you I needed you." Camille bit her lip to keep herself from saying more.

"I know, I know. You probably thought I was avoiding you. Especially after this morning." Paige's lips quirked. "About that…"

"No." Camille shook her head. "You were right. I was mothering you. Or"—she looked upward toward the ceiling—"smothering, as you called it. It's your body. If you want to—" She stopped herself from saying anything further. Like, *If you want to be stupid and do more damage to your body than you already have, it's your decision. Screw up another knee while you're at it, or your back or...* But if she said that, Paige would probably take off and she'd be stuck emptying the rest of the boxes herself.

"You're right. It is my body. And my pain." She placed her hand on Camille's arm. "Which means I know what I can handle and what I can't."

"Do you?"

Camille caught the slight flush to her sister's face.

"Okay, so maybe I tend to push myself too hard. But that's my choice, Cam. Not yours." A tinge of annoyance laced Paige's voice.

Camille breathed in deep and debated whether this was a fight she wanted to enter or if she should admit defeat.

Screw it.

"It might be your choice, but it affects us both. Affects our company. Our clients. Or do you not get that?" She swallowed the anger that rose with her words. "When you don't do your exercises, when you don't go to the doctor, when you don't take your medication…" She breathed in deeply, held it, and then breathed out again. "Paige, when you can't do your job, someone else has to, and I'm not sure if you've noticed, but we don't have any available hands at the moment."

"I can do my job." Paige dropped the wrapper she held in her hands and clenched her fists.

"Really?" Camille pulled out her phone. "Mrs. Wilson sent me a text yesterday. You forgot to stop by and look at her rosebush, which is dying. And the Andersons have been in twice this week to find out when you're going to go over and tend their gardens. Carla is getting quite anxious, since they have friends coming up from the city for the weekend. So guess what I was doing last night while you were God knows where?" She paused for breath and barely heard her sister's whisper.

"I was at the golf course."

"Of course you were." Camille shook her head in exasperation. "Where else would you be? Don't worry—I covered for you."

She pushed herself up from the stool and paced. The words poured out of her now that they'd started, and she couldn't have stopped herself if she'd tried. Paige just stood there, mute, eyes downcast, which irked Camille even more.

"It's not like I needed help with the delivery today"—her voice pitched higher as the words came out—"along with getting product ready for the booth at the beach or anything. It's a good thing I came in early—I had a feeling you wouldn't show up till later."

There was so much more she wanted to say but didn't. Things like, *Partners don't let each other down,* or, *We're a family and we need to start acting like one,* or like, *I'm here and I understand what you're going through.* She didn't say any of that because she couldn't.

It wouldn't make much of a difference anyway. Her sister liked to build up walls around her heart and pretend things were fine.

Fine. She hated that word.

It wasn't until Paige got up and placed her arms around her that she realized she was crying.

"I'm sorry, Cam. I really am. I should have been here; I just..."

Camille pushed herself away and swiped the tears on her cheeks away. She was an ugly crier, and she didn't need customers to see her with tearstained cheeks, red swollen eyes, and a nose to match.

The shop phone rang and Paige answered, giving Camille time to run to the back and splash water on her face. They needed to have a heart-to-heart talk about what was going on, about what was happening with the business and what it meant when Paige was never there to help out. They couldn't keep going on like this.

Paige rounded the corner. "That was Kaya." Kaya was their student employee who manned the booth down at the beach. "She's almost out of the little beach-supply baskets. I can't believe how well they're selling."

The supply baskets had been Paige's idea. Inside them were small bottles of suntan lotion, cream and gel to soothe burns, and moist wipes, along with a blowup beach ball, some toys to play with in the sand, and a gift certificate for a Still Bloomin bouquet or flower arrangement. They also sold bottled water, floppy sun hats, and flip-flops there as well.

"That's great. Good thing supplies arrived today." She pointed to a stack of six boxes in the corner. "I figured you could deal with those." She knew that sounded snippy.

There was a look on her sister's face that cut Camille to the bone: acceptance. She accepted Camille's anger and obvious resentment when she shouldn't have.

Camille wanted her to fight back. To argue with her like they used to, not wait for Camille to accept Paige's limitations. Just because her sister had destroyed her knee playing professional volleyball didn't mean everything about her was destroyed, and yet that was exactly how Paige acted sometimes. As if she were damaged goods.

Part of that might have been Camille's fault. Ever since their parents' death she'd taken on the mother role, forgetting she was only a sister. She'd done everything she could to help her sister heal from losing her dream of being on the Olympic volleyball team, to fill the void in her heart from losing her mother...but she'd only made things worse.

She'd slowly watched her sister's spirit disintegrate and she hadn't known what to do, lost to her own grief and the new responsibility laid on her shoulders—keeping the family business alive.

"Why don't we put some baskets together tonight?" Paige suggested, her voice meek, which only increased Camille's annoyance. What happened to her fiery sister who wouldn't back down from a fight, who knew what she wanted and never gave in?

"So you mean you'll actually be home? I'm beginning to wonder if you even remember where you live. I barely see you anymore."

Paige turned and focused on the boxes in the corner.

"Paige?"

"I've been housesitting one of the cottages." Her shoulder lifted in a shrug but she didn't turn around. "I thought I'd mentioned it to you."

Housesitting? No, she hadn't mentioned that at all.

"Whose cottage?" she barked. "Since when and for how long?"

"Listen, you're not my mother or my landlord. Back off." There was an edge to Paige's voice Camille hadn't heard in a long time, and it was nice. Even though it hurt at the same time.

"Back off? Seriously? That's not fair, Paige. I have the right to know when you're not going to be home." Camille's body tensed and her back muscles spasmed from the tightness.

"The right?" Paige finally turned around, her eyes blazing with fire. "I'll repeat myself in case you didn't hear me. You're. Not. My. Mother." She spat out the words.

Camille's lips thinned. "No, but I am the one responsible for you. The one who's been there through all your surgeries, through all your doctors' appointments. I'm the only one who is on your side, because I'm all you have left."

As the words slipped out, Camille realized she'd just crossed a line.

"Just like I'm all you have left," Paige said quietly, dousing the blaze of emotion Camille had been swept up in.

Camille bit her lip and nodded. She cleared her throat a few times before she could get the words out of her mouth.

"Can you"—she breathed in deeply—"can you at least let me know when you'll be home and when you won't be?"

"Seriously, Cam?" Paige sighed, folding her arms tight across her chest. "Last I checked I was an adult, which means I'm allowed to make my own decisions and live my own life. Sorry for not telling you I would be—"

"Late? Not coming home at all? Which one?"

Paige blushed. "Both. I don't need your permission, but you do deserve my respect. I'm sorry. I'll make sure I tell you in the future. Like tonight. I won't be home. I might not be home all week, so don't wait up for me, okay?"

Camille could feel her brows rise all the way to her hairline. "Not home all week? Do I ask where you will be? Or with whom?" She raised her hand. "No, don't answer that. You're an adult. You don't need to explain yourself or tell me where you are every moment."

Camille rubbed the back of her neck and forced herself to breathe through her nose. Relax. She had to relax.

"You're right." She held up her hands in mock surrender in an attempt to do exactly that. "You're an adult. Hands off—I got the message loud and clear." Her nostrils flared with anger she was trying really hard to suppress. "Do me a favor, though? Try to remember that we also work together, and I need to be able to count on you. So if you're not going to be in when I need you to be, send me a text, at least. That won't be too difficult for you, will it?"

"Fine," Paige agreed, her voice laced with tension.

"Fine," Camille repeated, feeling suddenly very childish. "I'll take my break when you get back from the beach," she called out over her shoulder before heading into their flower fridge. A little bit of distance could only help distill the tension between them right now.

"I won't be long." Paige opened the door to the fridge and popped her head in minutes after Camille entered. Camille's hands were full of assorted flowers she'd picked for an arrangement due in a few hours, and Paige eyed them. "How many arrangements are on the schedule today?"

"We have three for later this afternoon. Two deliveries, one pickup." Camille walked past her and placed the box of flowers on her work stand.

Camille nodded toward the order form she'd tacked to Paige's work board beside her. "Charlotte stopped by and placed an order for her mother. She wants to start up the weekly arrangements again."

These arrangements from Charlotte to her mother constantly changed. Doris would complain that Charlotte never sent her flowers and then complain that she sent too many, and the cycle repeated over and over.

"I wonder how long this will last." Paige loved to not only make the arrangements for Doris but to deliver them as well.

"I'll be back." Paige hefted into her arms a large box full of baskets for the beach stand. She headed toward the front door but stopped. "Cam? I really am sorry about not being here when you needed me."

Camilla made herself smile. What else could she do? For her, this shop was her life. It represented something deep and strong. Maybe it was because she'd been raised in here with her father, learning from him how to care for a community through her hands and heart. But Paige's dreams had been different.

She really couldn't fault her sister for not being here. Camille had to stop expecting her to be. Their mother used to call Paige her wild bird. She knew her younger daughter could never stay in one place for any amount of time, that she needed freedom to be herself, to try new things and to push beyond any boundaries laid out for her.

But that had all changed. Paige wasn't on the team anymore

and could barely walk without a limp on the best of days. She needed to do something with her life and seemed to take pleasure in the hands-on operation of the family business. She enjoyed being outside, working in the gardens, while Camille preferred to be in the shop, doing the day-to-day side of things.

They could do this—they could take the two things they both enjoyed and make it work in a way their father never could. They could expand their business, build on their name, and both find satisfaction with the life handed to them.

Right?

3

GRACE

THE SOUND of a dog barking in the distance startled Grace, and the knife in her hands slipped.

"Augh." She held her finger up and winced.

"You okay?" John stood at the counter.

"I'm fine. Thanks." The words rolled off her tongue without thought as she put pressure on the small cut and waited for the bleeding to stop.

John had come home a little later than promised, but in enough time to help with dinner, just like he said he would.

Except, since coming home, he hadn't said a single word to her until now.

"Can we talk now? Please?" She hated begging. Hated the way it made her voice sound, how it made her feel...and yet she'd prefer anything over his silence.

"You can't stay mad at me forever," she said. "You need to let me explain about today."

"Explain away." He took a drink from his bottle of beer and slammed it down on the counter.

Grace jumped.

"She's only a little girl. A baby." Why was he so upset about her taking care of Sophie? They'd had this talk countless times with always the same result: both walking away without ever coming to an understanding of where they stood.

She sighed.

John snorted. "You honestly can't think that's what's bothering me." The look in his eyes spoke of both pain and anger.

"Then what?" Grace cried out. "What else could it be? I don't understand what you have against her."

"I have nothing against her and everything against the situation you've been boxed into." John wouldn't look at her, only stared at the beer in his hand.

The doorbell rang.

Grace just stood there, waiting for her husband to explain, to maybe give her some clue as to how she could fix things, but he grabbed his beer and headed outside to the back patio, ignoring the doorbell altogether. Grace went to let her friend inside.

Dinner was awkward, to say the least. John continued to drink while Paige and Grace talked about the garden. The moment dinner was done, Grace began to clear the table.

"Here, let me help." Paige immediately stood. "Dinner was great; thank you guys for having me."

John leaned back in his seat and locked his arms behind his head, smiling for the first time that night. "Considering that you brought dessert, you're welcome to come anytime."

His words slurred slightly. Fabulous. He was drunk, or on his way.

Grace smiled faintly at her friend before she headed into the house and set the plates in her hands down.

"Everything okay?" Paige asked softly behind her.

Grace glanced through the open door toward her husband and sighed. "Things are fine. He's just…in a mood."

Paige set the items she carried down and leaned against the counter. "I've noticed. Want to talk about it?"

"Not really."

"Does it have to do with Sophie?"

Grace pinched the bridge of her nose. "What happened to not talking about it?"

"I have selective hearing." Paige winked.

"That little girl," Grace said, "is the sweetest thing in my life at the moment, and whatever mood my husband is in, it's because he chose to be that way."

"I can hear you, you know." John's annoyed voice startled both Grace and Paige.

"Sometimes the truth hurts." She said it quietly enough for only Paige to hear.

She would fight for Sophie all the days of her life if she needed to. It wasn't fair of John to put her in the middle of something that was obviously between them.

"Where's dessert? I'm still hungry," he called out as he leaned farther back in his chair to the point of it tipping and closed his eyes.

Grace closed her eyes and counted to ten.

"He's very demanding, isn't he?" Paige asked. She opened up the oven, where she'd set a warm apple pie when she first arrived.

"I heard that too." John laughed as if the idea of him hearing their conversation was the funniest thing ever.

Grace just tightened her lips.

Paige carried the pie while Grace grabbed the dessert plates.

"I'm sure our neighbors can hear you as well," she said to him as they returned to the patio. She attempted a smile, working really hard to add some lightness to her tone. She was not going to let him goad her.

John turned his head toward their friendly neighbor. "Hey,

Dale and Jenny," he called out, his voice loud and obnoxious. "We've got pie and wine or beer. You've got five seconds to respond or the offer's off the table." He laughed by himself while Grace and Paige just sat there. Eventually John shrugged when there was no response. "Your loss, my gain." He leaned forward and smelled the pie. "I probably don't want to share this anyway."

"Considering Anne Marie made it for you when she heard I was coming over tonight, I don't think you want to be sharing." Paige frowned as she slapped his shoulder.

"Never mind. Come over for beer later, Dale," John yelled over his shoulder with a smirk on his face.

"Okay," Dale yelled back.

Grace set a piece of pie on a plate and looked up, seeing Dale's silhouette in his kitchen window. She waved and he waved back.

"Unless you bought a new case of beer, I think that's your last one." She pointed the knife in her hand at her husband's bottle.

John winced.

"Ignore him." Grace continued to cut the pie.

"So you're still good for me to come tomorrow and start on your garden?" Paige rolled her eyes, not phased in the least by John's antics.

"As long as you agree to be on retainer to keep it growing." Grace liked the rough sketch Paige had drawn earlier. The idea was to keep it simple this year and build on it next year.

"So we'll actually have flowers and living plants?" John asked in between bites.

"Just help your wife water them in between my visits and they'll be fine." Paige winked at Grace.

"Don't even bother trying to shame me on this. You both know I don't have a green thumb." Grace sat and enjoyed her own pie. She made a mental note to call Anne Marie tomorrow to thank her for the dessert; she'd even added a hint of caramel that Grace loved.

"Want another glass of wine before you head home? We can go

in the house or sit out here and enjoy the night breeze," she asked Paige, who glanced at her watch.

"I'll take that as my cue to leave you to your girl talk." John said before walking away.

"Sorry about John," Grace said once they were alone.

"Don't worry about it. That's not the first time I've been around your husband with alcohol involved. Although, usually he's the fun one in the room...so this was a first. He wasn't that bad though, just... It's obvious something is going on between the two of you. Are you sure you wouldn't rather me leave?"

Grace shook her head. She was more than sure. "Not unless you really want to. I'm not keeping you from anything, am I?"

"I'm housesitting tonight," Paige said, "so other than watering plants, I'm good."

Grace sat up in her seat. "So you took Charlotte up on that offer? I didn't think you were going to. How's that going?"

Grace had been chatting with Paige one day downtown when Charlotte came by and mentioned that one of their summer families wasn't coming this year and needed someone to housesit. She'd asked them if they knew of anyone she could recommend and Paige had mentioned she might be interested.

But that was the last Grace had heard of it.

"It's a little bit of extra money, a really nice cottage, and it's nice, actually, being on my own. I used to daydream about having my own place, back when I was in the dorm at school. But then I moved home after my knee surgery and..."

"There's nothing quite like having your own space. I remember those days." Grace smiled. "Except I always had a roommate."

"Your sister."

"My sister."

They spoke at the same time before laughing.

"Are you there every night?" Grace asked.

Paige shook her head. "Just a few nights a week. I need to be home tomorrow to help Cam put some baskets together."

"Can I help?" The idea of doing something appealed to her. Normally in the summers she taught summer classes or volunteered with the children teddy-bear picnics held down at the beach. Her summers were always busy. Or they used to be.

"Really? Don't you have your hands full with Sophie, though?"

"Well…yes. But I'm all up for a girls' night. I'll bring the wine."

Paige looked surprised at her eagerness. "Okay, then. We've got a date. I'll let Camille know."

"What's this about tomorrow night?" John called out through the open kitchen window.

"Just a girls' night," Grace spoke up. "Gonna head to Paige's to help create some baskets. You don't have plans, do you?" She waited to see whether he'd respond, then shrugged, trying not to reveal her frustration. He could at least answer, especially when he was obviously eavesdropping. "Guess he's okay with it." Not that it really mattered. Their nights were quiet affairs lately. John would be holed up in his office while Grace read a book or parenting magazine. Always in separate rooms.

"No plans. Enjoy your night out. Maybe I'll head to down to Fred's for a beer and game of pool." John appeared with two wineglasses and a bottle of her favorite Reisling.

"Thank you," she said, registering his gesture. He gave her a smile before disappearing back inside, but it didn't take long for her to hear his voice through their neighbors' windows. He'd gone next door.

"Your birthday is coming up, isn't it?" Paige asked after a moment.

Grace nodded, sighing heavily at the thought. She'd rather hoped to ignore her upcoming birthday this year.

"Are you heading into the city for your annual trip with your sister or will she be coming here?"

And that was the reason why.

Her sister.

Before the shooting, she and Faith had talked daily, worked on crossword puzzles together via phone or text, made plans to see each other as often as they could, or Skype-chatted in the evenings.

Her twin sister was her other half, more so than her husband or even Katie.

Faith had always been the closest person in her life. But since the shooting Grace had kept her sister at arm's length.

From guilt. From grief. From... It didn't really matter the reason. She just had. She knew it was all on her, the distance that remained between her and her sister, but she wasn't ready to deal with it yet.

Much like a lot of other things in her life.

"Why do you ask?" Grace played with the wineglass in her hand, watching the liquid wash up the sides as she moved it around.

"With watching Sophie like you've been, I wasn't sure if you were actually going to get away or not," Paige said.

Grace took a sip of her wine, struggling with how to answer.

"I haven't really spoken to Faith about it." She looked out over her weed-filled yard and realized just how much it paralleled her life right now: Something that should be so beautiful was slowly choking to death. Her marriage. Her relationship with her sister. Her hopes and dreams for the future. Everything was slowly dying.

Fortunately there was hope for her garden.

For her...not so much.

"How is your sister?" Paige sipped her wine, but Grace caught her curious glance when she didn't think she was looking.

"I haven't really spoken to her."

Paige sighed. "You should."

She took a sip of her wine and avoided Paige's look. "My days are mainly full with Sophie, and..." Despite its being the truth, it still sounded like an excuse.

"You must really miss her, though."

Grace toyed with her wineglass. "Sure, I do. But we're both busy. She has her career and I have..." Her voice trailed off as she thought about all the things she didn't have anymore, like her baby, her best friend, her perfect marriage and perfect life. "It'll be okay. We've all got to grow up sometime, right?"

Paige gave a little laugh. "Yeah. Sometime." She blew a puff of air. "I think that's what Camille and I need right now."

"What's that?" Grace was more than happy to change the direction of their conversation.

"Some space. Time to grow and figure out who we are and... stuff. You know?" She downed the last bit of her wine and stood up. "On that note, I'd better get going."

"Are you okay?" Grace reached out, wanting to comfort her friend if she could.

"I'll be fine. Oh, I stopped by Nathan's today and weeded his garden a little. I found a cute marker beneath a pile of weeds in the back."

Grace stomach dropped. She knew exactly what marker Paige had found. "The one with the two old women?" She'd picked it at a garage sale and given it to Katie last year, along with a potted rosebush. The two old women on the marker reminded her of them, and she couldn't help but buy it. "Any roses still growing on that bush or are they all dead?"

"There were some buds. There's hope for it yet. I had no idea it was there." Paige gathered her purse and notebook. "It's hard to believe she's gone, you know?"

Grace swallowed hard. "I know."

She thought about it every day.

***

By the time John returned from having a beer—or two—with Dale, Grace had cleaned up the kitchen, folded a load of laundry, and was in her comfy night wear, curled up on the couch, flipping through the television stations.

John paused as he entered the room, almost as if surprised to find her there. "Sorry I was so long." He sank down on the couch beside her. "When did Paige leave?

Grace readjusted her feet to give him more room on the couch and shrugged. "Over an hour ago."

"You should have come over then."

She pulled her legs in tighter to her chest. "I wasn't in the mood to socialize."

"You never are anymore," John mumbled.

"What's that supposed to mean?"

He leaned his head back on the couch and closed his eyes. "Usually in the summer, by now we would have had a few barbecues with our neighbors, been on a few picnics, driven along the coast just to get away…and we've done none of that."

"Things are a bit different this year." Like she really needed to tell him that. Why did she have to explain or excuse herself? She couldn't just pretend their lives hadn't changed. That they were the same.

She couldn't ignore what had happened to them—losing their own child—and continue with life as normal.

Apparently he could. Or wanted to.

"How? We're still alive. We have a life that revolves around more than just this town and what happened here. Or at least, I thought we did."

Grace laid her head back on the couch and closed her eyes. "Are we seriously going to do this now? Again? Can we not go one week, or even one day, without having these talks about dealing with things and moving on?"

"Maybe if you would start to deal with things, then we wouldn't have to," John said.

She arched her brow. "We deal with grief differently. That much is clear." Hopefully one day he'd understand what that meant. "Stop trying to tell me how I need to handle things; stop trying to give me a time line...just stop, John. Please."

"Stop? I can't, Grace. We're in this together—at least, I thought we were. But you won't let me in. You've shut me out, won't talk about what's happened, and there's no way for us to move past this if we can't do it together."

The agony in her husband's voice sliced through her heart.

"We are in this together," she whispered. She opened her eyes to look at him, but he'd already turned away and stared blindly across the room.

"It doesn't feel like it, Grace. What happened to us, to our community, was horrific, but—"

Horrific? That was how he would describe it? Try devastating. Life altering. Soul crushing.

"I lost my best friend only a few months ago, John." She crossed her arms tight over her chest, a throw pillow held tight between her arms. "We lost our child. What happened didn't just happen to this town; it happened to us." Her voice broke. It was like he forgot that part, as if he glossed over her miscarriage and grief.

"You think I don't know that? That I don't live with that reminder every day? How do you think it feels to me to find someone else's child sleeping in the room meant for our baby? Or to see you hold Sophie in your arms, singing her a lullaby? Don't think I haven't noticed what you call yourself when you think no one is around."

"Call myself?" Grace was confused. She didn't understand why he was picking a fight with her—because it was obvious that was what he was doing.

John pushed himself up from the couch, his body suddenly rigid with anger. "Give me a break. As if you don't know."

She shook her head. "I have no idea what you're talking about. I call myself Auntie."

"You call yourself Mommy." His voice was low, almost a whisper, but held enough force that she felt like she'd just been sucker punched.

She grabbed onto the edge of the couch. "No, I don't." Her heart squeezed in pain. She wouldn't do that. She wouldn't betray Katie like that. She couldn't.

"I've heard you more than once."

She turned toward him, her body angled to his. "I wouldn't do that. Not to Katie." She searched John's eyes. Whatever she expected to see, sympathy or acceptance or even pity, it wasn't anger. Anger toward her.

"Not to Katie?" John stood, his fists clenched at his sides. "You wouldn't do that to Katie?" The way he said her name, with vehemence, shocked her. "How about you wouldn't do that to me, or to the child you lost? Why is it all about Katie?"

"Because it's my fault she's dead!"

The words rushed out before she had a chance to even think.

"My fault, John. Mine. It's because of me that she was at the school. If I had just gone to work like I was supposed to, instead of skipping town to see Faith, Katie would be alive. Her daughter wouldn't be motherless, and maybe, just maybe, our own child wouldn't be gone."

Tears filled her eyes, and she could hardly see John standing before her. She swiped the tears that ran down her face, and ignored the pain in her heart that threatened to crush her.

"Then you would have died." John stepped toward her, his eyes full of tears and love. "Do you realize that? You would be dead."

The anguish in his voice, the realization of his words, pulled at her.

"But at least she would be alive."

Survivor guilt. She'd never get past it.

"You don't know that." John reached out but Grace stepped backward, away from him.

"I do know. I would have done the same thing she did: stood in front of my students, protected them from harm. But I wish it had been me and not her. You would survive without me...but how fair is it that Sophie has to grow up without her mom?"

John shook his head vehemently. "I wouldn't—"

She fled toward their bedroom. How could he not understand? Sinking onto their bed, she clutched her legs tight to her chest.

It was something she and Katie had often discussed: the sacrifice of what being a teacher meant in the face of all the violent school shootings in their country. She thought about the seminars they'd attended in the city about recognizing the signs, being aware of issues before they occurred...but you never expected something like this to happen to you.

Katie was a hero. She'd put the needs of her students above her own, despite having a baby at home. Taking care of Katie's daughter, helping to raise her best friend's baby while her husband was grieving...it was the least Grace could do.

So what if it meant she and John didn't go out as much? Or they didn't go away like they used to? She wasn't the same person she'd been then. She'd changed. That moment the news came on the radio about the school shooting...she would remember it forever.

The stereo had been turned up, the window down, and there had been a happiness in her heart she knew now that she would never experience again. She'd been on her way to Seattle to spend time with her sister before John joined her and they had their own little weekend celebration: Grace was pregnant, a dream come true, and she couldn't wait to tell her sister.

She still remembered the spot in the road she'd been passing when the special bulletin came on. She was on I-525, between Freeland and Clinton. A little fruit stand stood on the side of the road, and the sign for the winery she and Katie loved to head to on weekends was just up ahead.

Time stood still when she heard. She pulled over to the side of the road, frozen. She would always remember that sensation of icy tendrils moving along her veins toward her heart from the tips of her fingers as they clutched the steering wheel. She'd gasped from the pain as she listened to the news: that one of the town's own had entered the school with a gun and shots were fired. Emergency vehicles were on the scene, but there was no word on what had happened after that. So she sat there, waiting, praying that this was all just a mistake, that what they thought had been a gun was actually something else.

She'd reached for her phone, her fingers fumbling with the device, and called her husband, but the line was busy. She tried again and again. She then tried calling Katie's cell, then Paige's, then John's again, but all she got were busy signals. So she sat there on the side of the road, tears streaming down her face, not knowing what was happening.

Moments later she'd wished to be back in that space of not knowing. Because the pain was nothing compared to finding out that there were casualties. Children. Innocent bystanders.

A teacher.

The moment she heard that, Grace turned her vehicle around, her body shaking, and drove back toward Stillwater Bay. To the nightmare that had now become her life.

She rocked herself on her bed now. She'd lost her baby within weeks of the shooting. The grief over losing her best friend, knowing it was because she'd asked Katie to cover her class that she was dead...Grace deserved what life had handed her.

How could she not help take care of Sophie? To love her and do what she could to ease Nathan's burden? Why couldn't her husband understand that?

Her cell phone rang. Her sister's name came on the screen, and without thought Grace hit the ignore button.

She wasn't ready to speak to Faith. Not yet.

A few moments later her phone buzzed with a text message.

I miss you. I have a week off and was hoping to come and see you. Please say yes.

Her chest tightened at the thought. When she didn't answer, Faith called.

Grace answered at the first ring.

"I can't." She barely whispered the words into the phone.

"I won't take no for an answer. I miss you. My flight is already booked and I'll be at your place before dinner." There was a note of pleading in Faith's voice, but Grace ignored it.

"No."

"No? You don't mean that, Grace."

She uncurled her body and stood, stretching her back, and then paced her small bedroom.

"Grace? Please don't do this."

Her fingers were freezing, so she placed the phone on speaker, set it down on the bed, and rubbed her hands together to warm them. "You can't just drop in like that." She couldn't handle her sister here. Not now.

There was silence on the line. Grace knew Faith was mulling over her words.

"Then meet me," Faith finally said.

"No."

"Then I'm coming." The pleading tone was gone. Now Faith just sounded frustrated and annoyed.

With her.

If anyone should be frustrated or annoyed, it was Grace. Who did her sister think she was?

She rubbed the back of her neck. "Now just isn't a good time, okay?"

"It's never a good time lately. What's going on? You won't talk to me anymore. You rarely return my texts, and this is the first time in over a month you've actually answered my call."

"You know exactly what happened."

"I'm coming tomorrow. Please be home."

Grace inhaled sharply. "I said no."

"I'm not giving you a choice." With that, Faith hung up, leaving Grace standing there in shock.

Did her sister just do that?

"Faith?" John stood in the doorway, his arms folded over his chest.

"She's coming tomorrow."

"I know."

Grace frowned. "You know?" She didn't like the sound of that.

He shrugged. "She asked what I thought about her coming for the week. I told her it was a good idea."

"She asked you first?" Her brow furrowed as she stared at him, daring him to look her in the eyes, expecting that he wouldn't. His gaze flittered about all over the room until he stared down at their carpet.

"John?" Grace asked again. "Since when have you started talking to my sister?"

"Since you stopped." He slowly lifted his head. "She's worried about you, and to be honest, she's not the only one."

"What's that supposed to mean?"

The look in his gaze was full of...compassion? Sympathy? Understanding? Sadness? She wasn't sure which.

"Whether you want to admit it or not, you need her. You won't open up to me; you won't go see a counselor. You need something or someone, and I hope to God she's it." He turned, as if wanting to leave, but Grace stopped him.

"John...I'm not..." She was afraid to admit that the idea of Faith coming scared her.

"Ready?" John looked at her, really looked at her, as if he could see into her soul. "Grace, it's time, don't you think? Time to stop running? What could happen that hasn't already happened? You lost your best friend. We lost our child. You lost a part of yourself you're afraid you can never get back; I get it. But none of that was your fault. I wish…" He stopped, and Grace almost thought he might cry. She started to get up, but he held his hand out to her. "You can't keep blaming yourself."

He left this time, and she listened to the echo of his footsteps as he walked toward his office.

She wasn't running. She was facing reality, and it was a lot harder than John obviously thought it should be. Reality was that she was childless. Reality was that her best friend's daughter was motherless. Reality was that school was going to start in a few short weeks and she wasn't as ready as she needed to be. Reality was…

Grace picked up her phone. *Don't come. I won't be here. I'm not ready.*

She didn't care what her sister thought of that text. And she didn't care what that meant about her own state of mind. If Faith did show up tomorrow…John would be the only one welcoming her.

She wondered whether they'd see the irony in that.

4

CAMILLE

Camille sat at the kitchen table, a hot mug of coffee in her hands, and blindly stared out the window of their cottage-style home. She hated mornings. Hated dragging her weary body out of bed, hated the pain in her feet as she made her way to the bathroom to shower while the coffee brewed nice and strong.

She felt like an old lady in a young*(ish)* woman's body. She was just barely pushing past thirty. As her father would say, *I'm getting too old for this.*

She smiled at the thought. Her father would mutter it every morning, and her mother would remind him he was only as old as he felt.

They died too young. They should still be here, working away in the flower shop, tending their own gardens, and living the life they'd always dreamed about. Instead, their lives had been snuffed out by a drunk driver a few years ago.

"I thought you'd be sitting on the deck." Paige shuffled into the room, her hair in a messy bun, wearing loose-fitting capris that barely hid her knee brace.

Camille yawned. "I can't seem to move from the chair. I didn't think you were going to be here?"

"I decided to sleep in my own bed last night." Paige poured herself a cup, stirred in some sugar, and then came to her, her hand out as if to help her sister up.

Camille lifted up her arm and then dropped it again. "Whose house are you sitting for, anyway?"

Paige yawned. "Oh, a summer family. The mayor mentioned that they were looking for someone to housesit here and there throughout the summer." She rubbed her eyes and yawned again. "They don't want people to think it's empty."

"Charlotte never said anything to me about it," Camille complained.

Paige shrugged. "I don't even really know the people, other than that it's a property Robert's company manages."

Camille frowned into her coffee mug. Her whole body lagged with lack of energy, and it even hurt to raise her arms to sip her coffee.

Paige pulled out a chair and sat. "Maybe you need to go back to bed? You don't look so hot. You're not getting sick, are you?"

Camille shook her head. "I can't get sick."

Paige's brow rose.

"We can't afford for me to be sick. You're busy with clients, which means there's no one to tend the store."

Paige laughed. The sound was bitter, full of sarcasm. "Are you serious? Life is not going to fall apart just because you're not there to hold it up."

Camille blanched as she realized how she'd sounded.

Paige leaned forward, her voice softer this time. "I'm pretty sure I can manage to keep our store running for a day. I can take care of our clients tonight; that's not an issue. You know that."

Camille sighed before yawning again. "Maybe I just need to sit outside. The crisp morning air usually helps."

"Or maybe go back to bed? You probably got one of those summer cold/flu bugs."

It was tempting. It really was, and it wasn't like there were a lot of orders today. Which meant she could relax a little at work, sit more than stand, and take it easy.

"I'll be fine," she said before another yawn happened. Tears appeared in her eyes from the exertion. Okay, maybe she wasn't fine. Maybe she should go back to bed.

"At least let me open this morning. Come in later."

That would work. She didn't need to take the day, just a few hours. Some extra sleep would be lovely. She was about to nod and tell her sister she would go back to bed, but she didn't get the chance.

"For Pete's sake, Camille. I wish you'd trust me a little. Don't you think it's time you let me grow up and be the adult that I am? You don't need to treat me like a little kid who only needs to water lawns and pull weeds. Stop being so damn controlling." Her sister's fingers turned white from the tight grip on her coffee mug.

Camille sat there, shocked into silence for a moment before recovering herself.

"If you want me to treat you like an adult, then start acting like one." With energy she didn't have, Camille pushed her chair away from the table and stood. "You want to help carry the load? Then by all means, do. But then you actually have to face life. Are you ready for that? Instead of hiding yourself at the golf course every day mourning over what might have been, it means you have to stop running from your past and get your knee taken care of. Pretty soon you'll be wearing those braces all the time. Should I get Dad's cane out of storage? Because you know that's the next step. The doctor has told you that over and over." She leaned down, her hands holding her weight against the table. "Being a grown-up means not running away from life. Are you ready for that?" She didn't wait for her sister to answer; instead she turned and slowly forced herself to walk toward her bedroom. Before she reached the door, she paused and looked over her shoulder.

"Thanks for opening up for me today. I'll try to be in by midmorning." She wasn't sure whether that softened the blow, but in all honesty, she didn't care.

She crawled back into bed and pulled the blanket up over her head. Normally after saying what was on her mind she'd worry about hurting Paige's feelings and try to backpedal. But today she didn't care.

Well, she did. But not enough to leave her bed and apologize. She spoke the truth. If Paige wanted responsibility, she could have it.

It irked her that her sister accused her of being controlling. Didn't she realize that Camille had to be? No one else had stepped up to take over, to carry the burden, to make sure they got through not only their parents' death but taking on a business. Paige certainly hadn't; in fact, until today it seemed like Paige hardly cared.

It wasn't like this was Camille's lifelong goal. Sure, she'd seen herself taking over from her parents when they retired, but that was later in life. She had plans. Plans to travel, to see the world, to build her own name as a garden designer. She gave all that up, though, after her parents' death and Paige's career-ending injury.

No one asked her and no one had needed to. She'd done the only thing she knew how. But apparently it wasn't enough.

Would it ever be?

* * *

BY NOON, Camille still hadn't left the house. Wrapped in a light cardigan with a blanket over her lap, she sat in her lounger on the back porch and wished the hot sun would warm her body. Her feet and fingers felt like ice cubes, and she kept having to wipe her eyes from tears that continually appeared with each yawn.

She'd slept for a solid four hours and yet she could have slept for another eight. Maybe she was coming down with something.

"Knock, knock."

Anne Marie came around the corner carrying a brown paper bag. "You know, for two women who love flowers and gardening so much, it always surprises me to see your backyard."

Camille smiled. Every single time Anne Marie came over, she said the same thing.

They lived in a cottage just off the South Beach, and other than flowering shrubs to separate them from the beach, they had only one rosebush.

Her mother had planted that bush days before she died, and Paige lovingly tended it and kept it thriving.

"Gina gave me a container of her chicken soup for you, and your sister tells me you still have some scones." She held the bag in her hand.

"There's one or two left from the dozen you gave us." Camille smiled and went to stand.

"No, no. Sit. I hear you're not feeling well." Anne Marie sat in the other lounger. "You never get sick, so for you not to come into the store means it's serious."

"I'm not sick." And again with the yawning. "Just exhausted."

"Which means your body could be fighting something."

"Or just that I haven't had enough sleep lately and I'm really tired." She reached for her coffee cup, only to remember it was empty.

"What's keeping you up at night?"

"Oh, you know, the usual stuff. Worrying about the winter season when sales will drop. Paige's knee is acting up but she won't do anything about it.... Just the same old things."

"You need to let this stuff go. I know, easier said than done, but it's not worth losing sleep over." Anne Marie carried her bag and Camille's empty coffee mug into the house but kept the back door open.

"Paige said to tell you things are slow but steady and not to worry, that she's got it all under control," Anne Marie called out.

"It'd be hard not to have it under control if it was slow," Camille muttered.

"What was that?"

"That's good," Camille said instead, her voice slightly raised.

"Sure. But then, it doesn't take much when the day is slow, right?" There was a chuckle to her friend's voice, loud and clear.

By the time Anne Marie came out from the kitchen with a tray in her hand, Camille almost felt warm. Almost.

There were two bowls of soup, two cups of coffee, and two scones slathered with homemade strawberry jam. Camille's stomach rumbled.

"I think I'm just exhausted." She smothered another yawn.

"Your body can only handle so much stress, girl. Why don't you take a few days off, let Paige handle things for a bit?"

Camille shook her head. "I can't ask her to do that."

"Why not?"

She had no idea, other than that it was highly unlikely her sister would be okay handing the store for more than one day. Paige had gardens to tend and couldn't do that if she was in the store all day.

She tasted the soup as a distraction and groaned. "Wow. This is fabulous."

"I know." Anne Marie leaned back in her chair. "I found out Gina's submitting her scone recipe for the fall fair this year, and you know I've won that award for the past three years."

Camille shook her head. "You guys never stop, do you? What you need to do is figure out a joint venture that complements you both rather than competing. It would make life so much simpler for the rest of us." She held the bowl of soup in her hands and let the heat of it seep into her skin. Why was she so cold?

"Where's the fun in that? We've had this rivalry since we were teens. By now it's become a tradition." She winked.

"I should probably call Paige to see how she's handling things, although no doubt she'll just roll her eyes and tell me to stop worrying." Camille sighed as she finished her soup. She was starting to feel a little bit better. Maybe all she needed was some homemade soup and a little rest in the sun.

"She's probably right."

"This is not where you get to say, '*I told you so*,'" Camille complained.

"Interesting." Anne Marie pursed her lips for a moment before taking a sip of her coffee.

"What?"

"Nothing."

Camille frowned.

"You're very defensive today. What's going on?" Anne Marie asked.

"Did you know Paige has been housesitting for one of the summer families? One of the cottages by the water."

"No, but that's nice, isn't it? Gives you both a little space and her maybe some extra income."

"Well, if you say it like that..." Camille mumbled.

Anne Marie's brows rose.

"Something is going on. She claims she told me about the housesitting, but I know she didn't. So while she's out sleeping comfortably in someone else's house, I'm pacing the floors wondering where she is. She's not exactly reliable lately, and I can't keep doing it all by myself." The words poured out of her, as if she'd been carrying the weight of worry for far too long.

"Is that what's keeping you up at night? Worrying about Paige?"

Camille played with the blanket covering her legs, tugging at the threads that had come loose. "Someone has to, don't they? I don't know how my parents did it when she was a teen."

"But she's not anymore. She's an adult."

Camille flinched at the words. Paige was in her twenties. She was definitely an adult, and yet…she would always be her younger sister.

"I know that," she said, her tone on the defensive side. "I do," she said more earnestly.

"You know, I love Sweet Bakes," Anne Marie said. "Starting up my own business was all I ever wanted to do, even as a child. I used to hold bake sales all the time, and my mom would sign us both up for baking lessons. But you… It has to be hard to be thrust into someone else's dream. Do you still have that scrapbook of all the places you wanted to visit? I remember you poring over that day in and day out, making a list of all the gardens you wanted to explore in France."

Camille smiled at the memory. "I dreamed of visiting Versailles and other châteaux, of seeing firsthand the amazing English gardens in Britain and walking through the Gardens of Augustus on the Isle of Capri in Italy." The longing was almost overwhelming. Would she ever see those places?

"It's hard to give up a dream, and must be even harder when you're forced to," Anne Marie said quietly.

Camille knew she was talking about Paige and her dream of being on the Olympic volleyball team.

"Why don't we plan a trip?" Anne Marie leaned forward, her eyes bright with excitement. "Give ourselves a year or two to save? I've always wanted to go to Europe and eat my way through Italy, savor the chocolate in Belgium, and eat a real fresh baguette in Paris."

Camille hesitated. "I don't know." She loved the idea, loved the excitement she could feel building up the moment Anne Marie suggested it, but…

"Come on, Cam. It's been your dream since you were a little girl. Think about it at least, okay?" Anne Marie suggested.

Camille nodded, a slight smile playing with her lips.

They sat there in companionable silence, something Camille loved that came so easily between them, until Anne Marie's phone chirped. She pulled it out and looked at it. Camille didn't think anything of it until she saw tears well up in her friend's eyes and her hand began to shake.

"What's wrong?" Camille swung her legs over so she sat facing her.

Anne Marie wiped the tears away and put her phone down. "Nothing. It's okay. Just a..." She sighed. "I had a reminder to take Bobby the antique car display in Oak Harbor this weekend."

Bobby had been Anne Marie's nephew, youngest son of her brother, Robert, and one of the victims of the school shooting. Jenn, Robert's wife, was a pillar in their small community, responsible for taking care of a lot of the volunteers, or had been until recently. Losing a child...that had to be the worst thing for a parent to ever experience.

Anne Marie rubbed her chest, as if massaging away the hurt. "It's only been a few months, but life goes on, you know. And at times you can forget...until something as simple as a reminder on your phone hits you hard."

Camille hadn't lost any family members in the shooting, but she knew what grief was. She glanced at the lone rosebush in her yard. Grief didn't go away just because someone said it was time to live life again.

"You never truly forget, and it's always the little things that remind you," Camille said quietly. Tears pooled in her own eyes and she wiped them away.

Anne Marie sniffed. "I should get going. I need to stop by Jenn's anyway before I head back to the store. We have some summer families coming in this week, and I don't have any information on them."

Stillwater was an ideal vacation town, located on Whidbey Island, just off the coast of Washington, and their population more than doubled over the summer seasons. Many families from Seattle owned a summer home here. The community liked to call them their summer families rather than simply labeling them vacationers.

"You're still taking care of the welcome baskets?" Camille asked. Every year their summer families would receive a small "welcome *back*" basket full of local produce and gifts, coupons for local businesses, and invitations to special events throughout the summer.

Anne Marie nodded. "Originally it was just to help Jenn out—she's still not ready to take it back—but you know, I kind of like doing it. It's fun, and I can see why she had a hard time giving it up."

"Some people cope in different ways, and even though keeping busy sounds good, when push comes to shove all it does it make you fall apart faster and harder." Camille spoke from experience. She would never forget those first few months after her parents' death…she'd been a wreck.

"Gina wants to host an end-of-summer luncheon, but I want to run it by Jenn first."

"Oh, I like that. Especially if you two are doing it together. Let me know if I can help in any way." She had some Stillwater signs for planters that she could donate.

"Well…now that you mention it, I had an idea." Not only was there a twinkle in Anne Marie's eyes, but she said it as if she knew Camille might not like her idea but she should.

Camille picked up her forgotten scone, bit into it, and almost choked as she listened to what Anne Marie had to say.

5

GRACE

THE WALKWAY to Katie's front door was cracked, and weeds protruded at an alarming rate. How many times would Grace have to remind Nathan to get it looked at? Katie would have been out here yanking on the weeds, filling in the cracks...anything to keep her yard looking welcoming and clean.

At least the gardens looked good. Paige did a great job keeping them weed-free. The yard had been Katie's pride and joy; she would be out here every morning watering her plants before sitting on her porch, coffee in hand and relaxing before greeting the day with a smile.

The memory hurt. Would that ache ever go away?

The sound of Sophie crying through the open living room window caught her attention and forced her to move beyond the past and into the present.

All night the memory of John's words haunted her. She called herself *Mommy* to Sophie. She'd not only betrayed Katie but also the child she herself had lost.

She loved Katie's little girl as if she were her own daughter, but she wasn't. Grace needed to remember that. She *had* to remember that.

Grace rang the doorbell, and Sophie's cries increased in volume.

The moment Nathan opened the door, he thrust his daughter into her arms.

"She won't stop crying." He looked ready to tear his hair out, and for a moment Grace was really worried.

"You should have called. I would have come over sooner," Grace said as she bounced Sophie in her arms. The little girl liked movement, whether it was being in a vehicle, going for walks in her stroller, or just being bounced slightly while being held…that and music calmed her.

Nathan should know this by now.

"I need to learn how to take care of my own daughter." He ran his hands through his hair, leaving the ends spiked, and sighed in frustration before turning to walk down the hallway, obviously trusting her to follow.

"I just put on a fresh pot." He filled two mugs, not asking whether she wanted one before he nudged her cup toward her.

With Sophie on her hip now, Grace raised her mug and took a sip, all the while noticing how Nathan watched her.

"I can't do that," he said.

"Can't do what?" She took another sip before placing the mug on the counter.

"Drink hot coffee with her in my arms. I'm afraid I'll spill it on her and burn her."

Grace smiled sadly. Katie would hate to see him like this, so insecure and uncomfortable around his own child.

Just another reminder of how Grace's decision had affected others in a powerful way.

She gently squeezed his arm before pulling a fistful of her own hair from Sophie's grasp.

Nathan stared at her, a blank look on his face.

"Are you okay?" she asked. She was worried. He seemed really off today, more so than usual.

"Will she even remember Katie?" he said softly.

Grace's breath caught.

"Of course she will." She would make sure Katie was larger than life for her best friend's daughter.

He shook his head as if about to say something more but stopped.

"So you said you needed me?" Grace asked.

Nathan had called her earlier that morning and asked whether she could come over. She'd just been about to leave; she had her bag packed, and even though she had no idea where she was headed...anywhere but home was the goal. She refused to be there when Faith arrived, but needed a reason other than that she was just *running away*, as John accused her of before he left for work.

Nathan scrolled through his phone. "I need to run to the office for a meeting with Arnold and..." He stopped and a haunted look crossed his face.

"What's wrong?"

He shook his head. "Nothing. I totally forgot about a golf tournament." He set his phone down and reached for an apple.

It took only a moment for Grace to remember: Katie had talked about going with him for the weekend with Sophie and taking her to see the Seattle Aquarium. Her friend had been quite excited about it.

"You're still planning on going, right?"

He gave her a look. "I can't take Sophie, and my mom is busy."

"I'll take care of her." She kept her voice calm, but inside she was jumping for joy.

"I can't ask—"

"You're not." Grace cut him off. "I'm offering. And it's perfect timing. John has some tight deadlines with work, so I'll stay here with Sophie and be out of his way. She'll probably appreciate sleeping in her own crib anyway, and I can crash on the guest bed."

She could see when the relief set in. Nathan loved his golf; Katie used to tell her that it was the one thing he liked to do where he didn't have to think about words or sentences or worry about keeping notes about potential article points. Golf meant relaxation for her husband, and Katie never had any issues with the amount of time he spent on the golf course, whether here or elsewhere.

"Are you serious?"

She smiled at him and gave Sophie a little kiss on the head. "Totally serious. Go. Get your stuff ready, talk to Arnold, and then get out of here. We'll be fine."

"Are you sure about this? John won't mind?"

Grace smiled and lied through her teeth. "He won't mind at all. In fact, it's perfect. I was going to ask if I could take Sophie on a road trip for the day to the petting zoo."

His facial features softened as he looked at his daughter. Grace could see the love he had for Sophie, and the yearning to be a good father. "She'd love that. Katie had a list of things she wanted to do with Sophie this summer and that was on it."

"She did?"

He nodded. "It's still on her desk. She labeled it her '*mother-daughter trips.*'"

"Then maybe you should be the one to take her." *I'm not her mother; I'm not her mother*, Grace repeated inwardly.

"I..." Nathan hesitated. "I want to, Grace. I really do. But what if something happens? What if she cries and I can't get her to stop? I'm not a good father; I know that. Not good enough to replace Katie." His chin lowered and for a moment Grace thought he was going to cry.

"You are a good father, Nathan. You are. You just need to trust yourself more. Katie would always go on and on about how awesome you were, how you would come home and take Sophie and soothe her...don't you remember that?" She leaned over slightly as Sophie reached her hand out toward Nathan. She set the little girl on the counter, holding her tight to steady her but giving her room to touch her father's hand.

Nathan stared at his daughter's small hand and Grace waited to see what he would do. She hoped he would take his daughter in his arms and trust himself, but instead he took a step back, stuffing his hand into his jeans pocket.

"Things are different now. Sophie knows that. She can sense it. She's great with you, but it's as if she can tell the moment you leave. It's like her heart is breaking all over again, knowing she's without her mom."

Grace swallowed hard. "I'm not her mom, though." Saying the words was hard. But she had to say them—to remind him and herself that she would never be Sophie's mother.

"You're the only mother figure she knows, Grace, and you have no idea how thankful I am for you."

Hearing those words was like a knife piercing her heart, while at the same time they comforted her, which didn't make sense in the slightest. And yet...for years she'd yearned to be a mother, and despite her miscarriage, taking care of Sophie, hearing Nathan say that... The bittersweet truth stung. She wanted to be a mother.

But not Sophie's. She could never be Sophie's mother.

"I can never replace Katie in your life—not yours or Sophie's. I wish..." She stared up at the ceiling and tried to stop the tears from forming in her eyes. "I wish I could have traded places with her, that I hadn't asked her to cover for me."

"I wish that too." His face blanched and he looked away immediately after saying the words. It was like they came out instinctively, as if it were a thought he'd had over and over and over and, while not meaning to actually say the words, he couldn't take them back.

"Grace, I..." Nathan shook his head and opened then closed his mouth, as if realizing there was really nothing to be said following his confession.

Grace was a firm believer of the saying, *Out of the mouth, the heart speaks.*

That kicked-in-the-gut feeling took over, churning from the pit of her stomach all the way to her chest, and it was all Grace could do not to fall apart. She blinked past the tears that formed and stared down at the beautiful little girl in her arms, a constant reminder of the pain and loss she'd caused.

When Nathan walked away, Grace stood there, mute. She wanted to call out, to say something, to apologize again, but couldn't. What more could she say? So instead she set Sophie in her high chair and scattered some dry cereal on the tray while she tidied the kitchen, anything to keep busy. There was a stack of flyers, pamphlets, and magazines on the corner of the counter that she straightened. One pamphlet in particular caught her eye.

Reverend Helman held sessions at the town hall every week for the victims of the school shooting. At the beginning, just after the shooting had occurred, a whole team of counselors had come and offered their services. Grace had even gone to a few sessions.

"Just throw those out if you don't mind." Nathan stood at the doorway, bag in hand, and pointed to the papers she held.

The mood between them was altered. Uncomfortable. She didn't know what to say, didn't know what she could say that hadn't already been said. A part of her wanted to leave, to walk away, but that would mean walking away from Sophie, and she'd already promised she would never do that.

"There are some parenting ones that look interesting," Grace said quietly.

Nathan only shrugged. "I need to get going. Thanks for…doing this."

She attempted to smile. She could pretend things were normal for Sophie's sake. She'd read that babies were tuned in to emotions.

"Before you do, I have a question. That city reporter stopped me the other day and mentioned that she wanted to do an article on Katie. She said that Arnold gave her my name."

Nathan winced. "Do you mind?"

"Nooo..." Did she? "I just wanted to make sure you knew." Which he apparently did.

He sighed. "Arnold sent me an e-mail a while ago. I gave your name. The idea is to draw attention to the community and the strength that Stillwater has, rather than letting it be a town people remember only by the shooting," he explained.

She bit her lip. "Do you honestly think that's possible? Why can't we just move on? Why do we have to keep reading about the shooting and everyone's speculations? Gabe is dead. He shot himself, and..." She stopped at the pained look on Nathan's face. "Sorry," she whispered.

"If it means people will remember Katie, if it will help to keep her memory alive, then I think it's a good thing." He looked at his daughter, then back at Grace. "I don't think that's asking too much, considering." The resolve in Nathan's gaze was strong and determined. "Is it?"

"Of course not." Grace cleared her throat. "Anything for Katie." Anything at all.

Even if it meant living with the knowledge that someone other than herself also placed the blame for Katie's death at her feet.

6

CAMILLE

WITH HER LEGS CROSSED beneath her, Camille turned the pages of her old scrapbook and let the nostalgia of memories ease her heavy heart.

Why couldn't she follow her own dreams? When had she decided her own life, dreams, and goals were less important than others'? As a child she would spend hours poring through magazines, reading articles about famous gardens all over the world. She'd dreamed with her father about visiting each of them, and had even made a list at the back of her scrapbook of all the ones they'd heard about. Her father had wanted to visit Russia to see the famous Peterhof and Alexandrovsky gardens in Moscow, and she even remembered him saying that would be his retirement gift to himself.

The more she thought of Anne Marie's idea about going on a trip, the more the idea appealed to her. With some careful budgeting, she might be able to do it in two years' time. If—and it was a big if—sales remained steady, and as long as Paige didn't need another emergency surgery.

"Hey." Paige pushed open the sliding door from the backyard. "How are you feeling?" She set a paper bag down on the kitchen table.

"Hi." She gave her sister a smile and patted the cushion beside her. "Better. I think a day of nothing but resting was exactly what I needed." Camille closed the scrapbook on her lap.

"Wow, I haven't seen that book in ages."

"I know. I started thinking about Dad and our talks of traveling the world together. Do you remember how he used to talk about that fountain in the Peterhof Palace gardens?" She remembered spending hours with him looking through magazines and online images of the gardens there.

For a moment her face was clouded in sadness. "Not really. Where is that?"

"Russia."

"Ah. Dad didn't talk about stuff like that with me. It was more your thing, right?" Paige came and sat down beside her on the couch, leaning in and resting her head on Camille's shoulder. "If you could go to one place within this book right now, where would you go?"

The question surprised Camille.

"Funny you should ask that." She rested her head against her sister's, thankful that despite the earlier tension, they could still sit like this, together. "Anne Marie wants to plan a trip." She lightly rubbed the cover of her scrapbook, interested in her sister's response.

"Cool. You going to go? I think you should." Paige sat up and patted her knee before jumping up from the couch.

"You do?" Of all the ways she'd imagined this conversation going—Paige feigning interest when she had none or a barrage of questions about finances and what would she do alone with the store—this was unexpected.

Paige shrugged. "Why not? You've always wanted to travel. Hey, I picked up dinner from Fred's. Chicken Parmigiana was on the menu. Hope that was okay?"

So like Paige to go from one conversation to another.

Camille's stomach grumbled as the aroma of one of her favorite dishes filled the air. "I thought we'd already used up our eating-out allowance for the week." While they were not on a terribly strict budget, it was tight, and Fred's wasn't cheap.

With hands on hips, Paige gave her a look.

"I'm just saying." Camille licked her lips while staring at the paper bag on the table.

"I'm aware of our budget. However, this was on the house. I stopped at his house today during my lunch and did some weeding."

"Sorry." She could see she'd crossed a line.

She's an adult. Treat her like one, Camille repeated to herself as she set the scrapbook to the side and stood, already salivating. "How about we eat out on the deck?" It'd been a while since they'd last sat down together for a meal.

They moved everything outside.

"This is nice, isn't it?" Paige mentioned after a few bites. "Two grown adults, who happen to be sisters, sitting at a table, enjoying a meal together. Treating each other as equals."

Camille got the jabs. She heard the admonishment. She could read between the lines.

"I said I was sorry," she reminded her sister. "You asked me to treat you like an adult…and I will. I promise."

"Thank you." Paige gave her a deep nod, as if accepting Camille's apology at face value.

"So," Paige said, setting her fork down after she'd finished eating, "back to your trip. You're going to go, right?"

It took Camille a few moments to respond. She thought long and hard about it, wanting to follow her dreams while facing reality.

She remembered something her dad used to say to her.

If you want it bad enough, you'll get rid of the excuses and start finding reasons to make it happen.

"I'm thinking about it." She stared out over their yard. "We should really plant something back here, you know?" While searching for her scrapbook earlier she'd come across a notebook she used for designing garden beds.

"We could." Paige followed her gaze. "Nice change of topic, by the way. Don't think I won't come back to it, though." Paige pursed her lips together as she looked over the yard. "How about you design and I'll plant? Is that what you're thinking?"

"Yeah. I just remember Mom saying she couldn't wait to retire so she could tend her own garden. She shouldn't have waited, you know?"

They both sighed in unison. It had taken a long time before Camille and Paige could talk about their parents without tears in their eyes. Now they could talk about their mom and smile sadly.

Her talk with Anne Marie had Camille thinking about a lot of things today. Looking back, she saw that her life was full of one regret after another. Regret over not pursuing love when she had the chance, of not traveling when she should have, of not telling her dad just one more time she loved him, of being angry with Paige over something she had no control over—mainly her knee and all the surgeries and their dwindling finances. Regret over not following her own dreams but feeling like she had to do what needed to be done, without thinking about herself first.

Maybe it was time to stop living like that. Maybe it was time to stop living in the past and start focusing on the future.

"They were always waiting for one thing or another," Paige said. "I know they gave up a lot for us, sacrificed a lot of their own dreams. Like Dad and his traveling, right?"

Camille gave her sister a soft smile. "It's not always bad to put others first."

"But you don't have to. Not all the time. When do we get to

start living the lives we want to live, rather than what others expect of us?"

Camille straightened at her sister's words. Funny how the very thing she'd been dwelling on all day came out of Paige's mouth. Like she'd been thinking about it too.

"Are you talking about the shop? You don't want to work there anymore?" she asked. It was like a knife piercing the center of her heart and twisting. That was their family business, something their parents had created to serve as their legacy. Was Paige wanting to throw it away?

"This isn't the life I thought I'd live, you know?" Paige winced and rubbed her knee. "I realize I can never play volleyball again, but I never really thought about afterward. Eventually I knew I'd have to do something with my life; this just wasn't what I had in mind." Paige looked out over their yard, the look in her eyes faraway.

"I'm sorry." Camille wanted to lean over and give her sister a hug. She knew how hard giving up her dream had been for Paige, how devastating it was to find out she'd never play again.

Paige shrugged. "It is what it is. But there's nothing for you to apologize for." She leaned forward and rested her elbows on the table, her face soft but her gaze strong. "I was thinking about it today actually. I hated sitting inside all day, waiting for people to come by, and yet I know you love being there. There's history in there for you, memories of our parents that seem to feed your soul."

Camille swallowed past the lump in her throat. "What is it you want to do then?" She wasn't sure how she could run the business by herself.

"I like what I'm doing right now. Being outside, tending the gardens, weeding other people's flower beds...it's actually soothing to my own soul. Surprising, huh?" She rubbed her knee. "A killer for this, though. Maybe it's time I went back to the doctor."

For a moment Camille couldn't breathe. Had she heard right? Paige not only liked working in the gardens, but she was going to get her knee taken care of? Miracles did happen. The tight feeling in her chest eased and she breathed a sigh of relief.

"For a moment there I thought you were telling me you were done." She reached over and grabbed her sister's hand, squeezing it with happiness. "I thought you were going to leave me, tell me you wanted to do your own thing, start a new life, live a new dream. I can't tell you how relieved I am right now."

Paige squeezed her hand back.

"I'm not leaving, Cam. We're in this together." She looked off into the distance. "We just need to figure out how that works, for both of us."

"You're right," Paige began. "It's time we talk about what our new dreams should be."

"But?" There had to be a but in there somewhere. Camille gripped the chair handles and squeezed.

"But I…I think my first step should be finding my own place to live."

The breath Camille held caught in her throat, choking her. She coughed, unable to breathe in, unable to ask the questions that were there on the tip of her tongue.

Paige jumped from her seat and pounded Camille's back, as if that would help to open her airway.

When the shoe dropped, it dropped. This morning Paige accused her of not treating her like an adult, so what did her sister do? She made sure Camille had no choice but to see her as one.

Once she could breathe, Camille leaned back in her chair, head dropped back, and stared up at the sky.

"Cam?" Paige stood at her side, concern filling her face.

"I'm okay, I'm okay." She pushed back her chair and stood. "So…moving out huh? Wow. Did not see that one coming." She walked into the house, Paige trailing behind her.

"You're not mad, are you?" Paige asked.

Camille stood at the counter, her hands gripping the edge, and counted to five, nice and slow.

"Of course not," she said. "Surprised, but not mad. Is this sudden or"—she turned to face her sister—"something you've been thinking of for a while?"

Treat her like the adult she is. Treat her like the adult she is, Camille repeated in her head.

Paige shrugged and ran her fingers through her hair. "It just feels…right. Like it's time, you know?" She stared at Camille, pleading with her eyes for understanding.

Camille was reminded of a similar conversation she'd had with her own mother, years ago, when she'd first broached the idea of moving out and living on her own. *Spreading her wings,* so to speak.

"When I was ready to move out, Mom and I stood here, almost in the exact same spots. I told her it felt like it was time too." She smiled sadly at the memory.

"What did Mom say?" Paige leaned against the table and waited.

"That I would be the only one who knew when it was time or not, that I needed to trust my own instincts. She offered to take me shopping for towels and sheets and kitchen stuff." Camille swallowed and breathed in deeply. "She then said that while I might think it was time, for her there would never be enough."

When she glanced up, she caught the sheen of tears in Paige's eyes before wiping her own.

"I guess I feel that way right now. I'm…I'm going to miss you, you know?" Camille admitted.

Paige rushed over and wrapped her tight in her arms. "It's not like I'm going far."

Her sister smiled through her tears, which had Camille fighting her own even more.

No matter what came their way, no matter how many times

they butted heads or argued, Camille would forever be thankful to have her sister by her side.

Even if that meant learning to let go just enough for her sister to find her own way back home.

7

GRACE

For the past hour, Grace had ignored both her husband's and her sister's multiple texts.

Where are you? When are you coming home? Your sister is here. You are coming home, right? Damn it, Grace, where are you?

I'm here. Stop running away from me. Grace, don't shut me out. Please, I miss you. Tell me where you are and I'll meet you.

She hadn't responded to either one of them. Nor did she plan to.

Except...she knew that wasn't fair to John. She could at least let him know she was okay, even if she wasn't coming home.

Her sister...that was another story entirely. It wasn't that she didn't want to see Faith, but whenever she thought of her, she thought of Katie.

Not just Katie, though. The way the air had crackled with tension as emergency vehicles surrounded the school, the static sound of the police radios, the frantic cries of parents as they embraced their children, and the screams of those who couldn't.

She would never forget the sound of the ambulance door slamming shut before it drove toward the hospital, or the way the wheels of the gurney squeaked as Katie's cold body had been rushed through the hallway.

Nor would the memory of her students who rushed toward her ever leave. *Mrs. Bryar, you're safe,* they'd said. *Safe.* Whereas their other teacher was now dead. Dead. Because of her. Because she'd taken the day off to see her sister.

If she hadn't, if she'd agreed to see Faith in the evening, after work, Katie would still be alive. Here to raise her daughter. But Grace had put her desire to see Faith first, and thus Katie's life last.

She would never forgive herself for that.

Sophie fussed in her arms from a slight fever but finally fell asleep as Grace rocked her. She slowly placed her down in her crib and crept of out the room, where she took in a few deep breaths and forced the memories away.

To pass the time, Grace curled up on the couch, a glass of homemade iced tea she'd made earlier beside her, and she reached for a parenting magazine Katie had subscribed to before she stopped. It felt odd to be staying here in Katie's home, especially now.

Her phone rang, and out of habit, because Sophie was sleeping, she answered it.

"Please tell me you're okay."

John's worried voice hit her hard, and for a moment Grace felt guilty for not responding to his texts.

"I'm okay."

"Thank God. I've been worried. It's late; where are you?"

She glanced at the time on her phone. It was late. Just after eight o'clock. "Is Faith at the house?"

"She's waiting for you."

Grace bit her lip in frustration. "Then I'm not coming home. I told you that." She flipped pages in the magazine without really looking at them.

John sighed. "Where are you?"

The baby monitor beside her crackled with rustling from Sophie. Grace waited to see whether she'd start crying, but blissful silence was all she heard.

"What was that?" John asked.

Grace got up and made her way out to the backyard. She pulled a chair away from the patio table.

"It doesn't matter, John. I'm fine, but I'm not coming home while Faith is still there."

She forgot that Sophie's window was open and didn't keep her voice down. Within seconds Sophie's cries could be heard.

Grace sighed.

"Is that her? Sophie? Are you kidding me?" John swore beneath his breath, surprising Grace. "You're at his house?"

"It's not like that." The moment he swore, she realized he must be thinking she was staying here with Nathan and she felt sick to her stomach. "He's not here. He went to play golf at a tournament for the weekend."

"That doesn't change anything. You ran from me to him."

"I ran to her. Sophie. To be there for Sophie." She needed him to realize that.

"To play mommy?"

"What? No! John..."

He laughed, the sound grating. "I might be a little slow, but I'm finally seeing things for how they are. First I find out he comes to the house when I'm not home and now you're staying there. Is this what you want, Grace? You want to make up for what happened so badly that you're willing to..." His voice petered out and Grace fought to breathe.

"No, John, no. It's not what you think. Sophie needs me. He needs me. I just... This is all my fault and I..." How could she get him to understand when she couldn't even say the right words?

"What about me? What about what I need? What about our marriage and our life and everything we've been through together? You're okay to throw that away, just like that, because Nathan needs you?"

She shook her head. It wasn't like that.

She'd go home. She'd pack up Sophie and head home and try to get John to understand.

"I'll come home." Sophie was awake anyway, or at least she had been. She wasn't crying anymore, but it didn't matter. She suddenly felt panicky to get home and fix whatever had just happened between her and John.

"No, don't. I wouldn't dream of forcing you to do something you didn't want, like coming home where you belong." There was coldness in his voice that intensified the fear growing in the pit of her stomach.

"John, I'm sorry," she tried again. "I came to see if I could take Sophie to the petting zoo, and Nathan mentioned the golf tournament and..."

"And you thought it was perfect timing. Except you didn't bother to tell me, and let me get worried when you wouldn't respond to any of my texts or calls. Doesn't that tell you something, Grace?"

She looked around, at the darkening sky, and shivered.

"I'm sorry." She let out a long breath.

"So am I. What's happening to us? Ever since the shooting you've pulled away from me, from us. I miss you." His voice broke. "I just want my wife back. The one before all of this happened to us."

Being sucker punched right in the gut couldn't hurt any worse than his words did.

"I just want my baby back. But we all can't get what we want, can we?" The bitterness in her voice came through, and while she knew she should have bitten her tongue, for some reason she couldn't.

"That hurt," John almost whispered.

"I will never be that woman again, John. There is no going backward." No matter how much she wished it.

"No, but you don't seem to want to move forward either."

She heard the frustration in his voice and understood it. She was just as frustrated. So where did that leave them?

"I didn't just lose my best friend. I lost our child." Why did she have to remind him of this; why did she have to keep saying this before he'd understand? "I lost my dreams and hopes, and it was because of something *I* did." Her whole body shook.

"I was the one who got Katie killed. No!" She stopped him before he could even argue with her about this. "I know what you're going to say, because you say it every single time. This is something I need to work through, and it's going to take time." She sighed and leaned back in her chair, tears streaming down her face. "Maybe you can get past the loss our town experienced. Maybe you can forget that we lost our child...but I can't. Stop expecting me to deal with things as fast as you have." She paced the backyard, walking along the patio and onto the grass. She kicked off her sandals to feel the strands between her toes.

If she didn't hold on to her grief, then that baby they'd lost would be forgotten.

"Who said I've dealt with it? You think I've forgotten what happened? The pain you were in when you collapsed and had to be rushed to the hospital? I thought I'd lost you, Grace. You talk about wishing it had been you, of trading places with Katie, and all I can think about is the fact that I'm glad it *wasn't* you." He stopped and there was silence between them.

"I know it's wrong of me to be glad you weren't the one at the school that day, and yet I won't take it back. The worst thing I can imagine is losing you, and that's where we're different, aren't we? Because for you, the worst thing has been being alive." His voice was low as he said the words.

"What do you want from me, John?" She forced the words past

the lump in her throat. She couldn't change how she felt. She couldn't get rid of her guilt or wishing things had been different.

"The only thing I'm expecting from you, Grace, is to be there. With me. But you aren't. Your whole life revolves around Sophie, because you feel guilty."

Grace gasped. "Of course I feel guilty. But that's not why I'm here with her. I love her. She's innocent and precious and doesn't deserve to be affected by the nightmare we're all living. She deserves to feel the love of a mom in her life."

"But that mom isn't you," he said quietly.

She trembled at his words and felt her heart tear into small pieces.

"I know," she whispered.

"If you know that, then why are you there when your home is here? You could have brought her here. So I need to ask you a question."

Grace waited, dreading the words she was about to hear.

"Is it love for Sophie or her father that has you there?"

How could he say that? How could he ask that? He should know...he should know.

"But I don't," John said softly, his words piercing her heart.

She hadn't realized she'd said that out loud.

"I love you, John. You. Only you. Nathan doesn't even... He's not even part of the equation here." She really needed him to understand. "Everything I've done, everything I'm doing...it's for Sophie." She swiped at her cheeks, the palms of her hands wet from her tears.

It killed her inside to know her husband doubted her love for him. Killed her. The problems they'd been having, she thought they could work through them, that they remained unbreakable... but if he doubted her, doubted their love...

Oh, God, what had she done?

* * *

"Faith!" Grace opened the front door in surprise. She was in the middle of getting Sophie's bag ready to head home and talk to John when the doorbell sounded.

The change in her sister startled her. She was thinner, with an almost gaunt look to her face. There were dark circles beneath her eyes, and her hair was in a messy bun.

Faith's hair was never messy.

"I figured if you weren't going to come to me, I'd come to you." Faith stood there, hands clasped tightly.

"I was just on my way home."

Grace went to take a step backward but stopped, remembering she'd set Sophie's carrier behind her earlier, which left Grace with nowhere to go once Faith's arms wrapped around her in a hug.

"I've missed you, Grace," Faith said softly.

It took a few seconds, but Grace's body relaxed and she raised her arms to hug her sister back. "I told you not to come," she reminded her. But now that she saw her, she was so glad to have her here.

Faith shrugged. "I decided not to listen."

"Did John send you?" Grace let her arms fall.

"No. It was my suggestion. I offered to come and spend time with the baby so you could go home. You guys have some things to talk about."

Grace crossed her arms. "I don't need marriage advice from you."

"Of course not, sorry. I just...I can't seem to say anything right with you lately." Faith rubbed the back of her neck.

Grace turned, grabbed the car seat, and walked into the kitchen, where she unbuckled Sophie and held her close.

Faith followed close behind. "I'm also here to talk."

"There's nothing to talk about."

"Your avoiding me says otherwise." Faith held her finger up for Sophie to grab hold of and smiled as the little girl reached out for her.

"Can I?" Faith asked, her own arms outstretched.

With reluctance, Grace relinquished her hold and her stomach twisted as she watched her sister interact with Sophie.

Faith would have made a wonderful aunt.

"I'm sorry, Grace," Faith said, as if reading her mind. "I know I've said it before, but I can't say it enough: I'm so sorry that you lost your baby. I know how excited you were."

"It was my own fault," Grace said quietly. "Nothing for you to be sorry about."

Grace jumped as Faith touched her arm. "You can't believe that. It wasn't your fault you had a miscarriage."

Grace shook her head in disagreement and looked away. Faith didn't know, didn't understand.

"Then tell me."

Startled, not realizing she'd said that out loud, Grace turned around and stared out the large kitchen window.

"It's not just about losing our baby, Faith. It's about everything else. That little girl you're holding is proof of it all; she's…she's the symbol of everything I've lost. I…" Her throat tightened, "I shouldn't be here. I shouldn't be the one caring for her, but it's because of me, because of you, that I am. We're the reason Katie is dead." She turned around to face her sister, taking in her pale face at Grace's words.

"It's because of you that I'm still alive. You know that, right? If you hadn't called and mentioned that you were in the city, if you hadn't talked me into taking the day off, I'd never have called Katie to take my class. I would have been the one there with my students, protecting them, dying for them. Me." She pounded her chest hard. "Katie would still be alive. She'd be here to take care of her baby, to build a family with Nathan, but I took that away." She crossed her arms tight over her chest. "We took that all away from them."

Her voice broke and the tears fell. Guilt, anger, and sadness hit her hard, and she crumpled to the ground. With her knees pulled tight against her chest, she hid her face between her arms and cried, sobbing as if her whole world had just collapsed.

Faith was beside her, holding her close, and when she looked up she noticed Sophie on the floor with them as well, safely tucked into her car seat.

Grace rested her head on her sister's shoulder, her breath ragged as she struggled to pull herself together.

"Have you been holding that in all this time?" Faith said. "No wonder you're a wreck." Her sister's hand rubbed her arm soothingly. "It's not fair, you know. You…" Faith sighed. "I love you, sister, but it's time for some tough love, whether you want it or not."

Grace pulled back. "What are you talking about?"

Faith stood, leaning against the counter, her arms crossed over her chest. "Grace, honey, I'm so glad you asked that. I love you. You know that, right?"

Grace nodded.

"Good. So, blame me all you want; I'm okay with that, now that I understand what's going on. But this whole"—she drew circles in the air with her finger—"martyr thing? This isn't you. Do you think Katie would like seeing you like this?"

Faith began to pace back and forth across the kitchen floor. "Let me answer that for you," she continued. "She wouldn't. Nor does your husband or anyone else who is close to you. This isn't you."

Grace snorted. Faith had no idea who she was anymore.

"What happened to the woman who looked for the bright side of things rather than focusing on the dark? What happened to the woman who lived her life with the challenge to make the world a better place? Is she lost?" She stopped when she reached Sophie. Faith bent down and gathered the little girl in her arms.

Grace wanted to stop her, to take the baby from her and hold her close to her own chest.

"What about your students, Grace? Have you thought of them in all of this? Are you spending any time this summer like you have in the past taking part in those teddy-bear parties on the beach or hosting tea parties at your house? Or are you only focused on this little one?"

Grace staggered back, horrified at the portrait her sister just painted with her words.

"How can you say that? You have no idea what I've been going through. None."

Faith hadn't been there. But Grace had been. She felt like she was still there. All it took was a moment of weakness, of letting her guard down, and the memory of that day hit hard.

After Katie had been taken away in the ambulance, Grace stumbled around, unsure of what to do, where to go. She saw the looks on people's faces, the disbelief, the fear, the horror, and she was helpless to help them in any way.

She'd begged one of the officers, a father to one of her students a few years ago, to let her into the school, saying that the children needed someone familiar when they were found. She'd walked through the hallways beside the police and paramedics, looking for her students, calling out to them, letting them know everything was okay now.

She came upon a closed closet door beside the girls' washroom. She remembered looking back down the hall, where all the other doors were open. Grace could still see her hand reaching out toward the doorknob, could remember the way it shook as she swung it open to reveal little Ellie Thomlin huddled in the far corner, hands pressed hard over her ears.

"Oh, honey!" Grace stepped in and bent down, careful not to

scare the little girl. "Ellie, it's okay now," she said as she reached for the Ellie's hands and gently pried them from her head.

"Mrs. Bryar?" Ellie's voice was shaky. "Mrs. Bryar, I'm scared." She launched herself into Grace's arms and wrapped her hands around Grace's neck, almost knocking her over in the process.

"I know, honey, I know. But it's okay now. Everything is okay now," Grace repeated over and over as she stroked the girl's hair.

Numb and needing to remain strong, eventually Grace was able to coax Ellie out of the closet, and hand in hand they made their way down the hallway and to the main front doors, where Ellie's mom, Lauren, stood with a group of other mothers. The moment Lauren caught sight of her daughter she ran over, dropped to her knees, and held her daughter close to her chest, tears streaming down her face as she realized her child was alive.

Grace's heart still ached at the memory of relief on Lauren's face. Just as it ached as she thought about the way Nathan had looked when she found him.

Katie.

That was all he'd said. One word. His wife's name.

But in that word everything he felt could be heard. Anguish. Disbelief. Anger. Heartbreak.

Grace couldn't say anything. There were no words.

Charlotte Stone had come up to them and placed a hand on Nathan's arm. She spoke the words Grace hadn't been able to say.

"I'm so sorry, Nathan."

"How could this have happened? How?" Nathan shrugged off Charlotte's hold and turned to Grace. "She wasn't supposed to be there. She. Wasn't. Supposed. To. Be. There," he yelled at her.

Grace could only shake her head.

Still, to this day, the look in his eyes, the hatred, the accusations... they were still there. She could still feel it radiating off of him every time he handed Sophie to her, every time Katie's name was mentioned. He blamed her...and he had every right to. Every right.

"Talk to me!" Faith's voice jolted her from the memory.

"You have no idea," Grace said. "No idea what I'm going through. No idea what it was like that day to face my students and their families. To stand with them afterward trying to comfort them, to help them make sense of the horror they'd just lived through. You have no idea what it was like to attend the funerals of those ten children who died, or to watch as my best friend's body was laid into the ground, knowing I was to blame!" Grace's body shook from the anger that coursed through her.

"You're right," Faith said softly. "I have no idea what you went through—because you shut me out, and I let you. I let you because I knew it was what you needed. You needed someone to blame, someone to focus your anger on instead of yourself."

Grace's hands fisted. "You think I blame you? Not as much as I blame myself." She kept her voice steady and almost emotionless. "I didn't have to leave that morning. I could have waited till my classes were over. I could have told you to have fun shopping until I arrived. I could have done any number of things that day, but I didn't. I jumped at the chance to spend the day with you because I had news I wanted to share."

"Oh, Grace." Faith sighed. "The only one to blame here is the teenage shooter. Gabriel Berry. He's the one who made the decision to enter the school with a loaded gun. He was the one who pulled the trigger and shot all those students and Katie. Him. Not you. You didn't kill her."

"I might not have pulled the trigger," Grace's voice shook. "But it's my fault she was there. It should have been me. Don't you see that? It should have been me protecting my students, putting their precious lives before mine." Her voice hitched and she turned to stare at Sophie, whom she realized was happy and content for the first time in a long time.

"This little girl is going to grow up without Katie and it's because of me. You and John think I'm running away, that I'm living in denial, but I'm not."

"Then what are you doing, Grace? Tell me!"

The sadness in her sister's voice brought the tears Grace had wanted to squelch. She couldn't. They welled up until she couldn't see clearly.

"I'm trying to live with the heavy burden. I'm trying to live knowing I killed my best friend. Not the kid who took the gun to the school and lost control. Me. Because I placed myself first, my needs before my duties. My fault." Her fist hit the counter hard with those last words and she swore at the pain that flared up.

"Grace, it's not your fault. You can't blame yourself. You can't. It's eating you up inside." Faith's eyes were so full of love, of compassion. There was no blame. No anger. Nothing but love.

In that moment, when all Grace felt was sadness and grief, little Sophie laughed. Her voice, pure and innocent, filled the air, and all Grace could do was stare at her.

"You love her, don't you?" Faith said.

"So much. But not as much as her mother did."

"You can't carry that burden, Grace. It's going to destroy you," her sister said quietly.

Grace didn't say anything; she couldn't. Destroy her? It already had. She was merely trying to pick up the pieces.

8

CAMILLE

"HEY, LOVELY LADY."

Camille opened the door to Stan's gentle voice. Her deliveryman was here with her weekly floral delivery.

"Good morning, handsome." She wedged in the stopper for the door to remain open and then stepped to the side.

"Now, now, don't be saying things like that. If my wife found out, she'd stop sending you her special teas," Stan teased as he hefted a large box in his arms through the door and set it on a table.

"We can't have that, now, can we?" Camille reached for a bag she'd set to the side. "You'd better take this, then, and give it to her."

She'd never met Stan's wife in person, but that hadn't stopped them from connecting and building first a working relationship and now a sort of friendship. Stan's wife supplied tea and made homemade items while Stan drove a delivery truck to local florist shops on Whidbey Island.

"Do I dare ask what it is?" Stan took the bag and peered inside.

"Just a little thank-you from me to her for the extras she always adds with my order. Don't think I haven't noticed."

"Well, then, you'll really like what she placed in there today." Stan winked before he left to retrieve buckets of flowers Camille had ordered.

Interested, Camille opened up the box and found it full of the regular items she ordered, loose teas wrapped in both individual and larger packets, a few really cute mugs to go along with them, and some tea-infused soaps and creams. But at the bottom was a gift-wrapped box with her name on the tag.

"It's to celebrate the anniversary," Stan said.

Understanding dawned a few moments later. It'd been a year since she'd started ordering and displaying their teas and gift items.

"It's been a very good year, hasn't it?" Camille took out the box and unwrapped it. Inside was a teacup and infuser, but when she looked at the teacup better she went over and gave Stan a hug.

"You make sure you give that sweet wife of yours a hug for me, okay?"

The cup was beautiful. It was soft blue in color with a floral design, but the words touched her heart.

The most beautiful of flowers grow out of the darkest of moments.

"It's lovely." Camille loved the cup and would use it daily, as a reminder that life didn't stop after tragedy.

Stan gave a deep nod. "She thought you would like it. She had an idea of making some cups with that saying, and perhaps even some signs, if you were interested. She wasn't sure whether it was too early or not."

Camille thought about it for a moment. "I don't think so. In fact, what if you were to make some smaller signs that I could stick in some flower baskets instead? And the larger ones we could sell next door?"

The Treasure Chest, the store that belonged to Julia Berry, the mother of the teenage shooter, had closed after the shooting occurred. It was a source of income for many in the community who sold locally made items, and now it was open again, thanks to Mayor Charlotte's help. She'd found some volunteers to help not only keep it open but keep the product moving until Julia felt like she could take over again.

Camille had no idea how long that would last. She'd been by Julia's house a few times with flower deliveries, but the grieving mother wasn't quite ready for visitors. Not that Camille blamed her. The media, when they'd literally been parked out on the streets of Stillwater in May and June, had vilified her, and not many had stood up to help.

One of Mayor Charlotte's goals was to revitalize their town after the shooting, to be a strong community, and one way of doing this was ensuring that all their stores were open for business and their town was moving forward. It was a slow process, but they were getting there.

"You think so?" Stan shuffled his feet, looking slightly embarrassed. "I have a few samples with me if you want to see them."

"Absolutely. I'm glad you thought to bring some with you." Every so often Stan would bring some homemade items for her to look at, and she'd either offer to sell them in her store or take them next door.

Once all the flowers were in the fridge and Stan had gone to continue his deliveries, Camille took a look at her calendar to see what was on the schedule for the day. Paige had made some notes for arrangements due later this afternoon, but Camille wasn't sure whether she planned on making them herself or if she should go ahead with them.

She hadn't seen her sister since learning Paige planned to move out. After their talk, Camille had basically hidden in her room, trying to absorb the idea that her sister was going to leave her. She wasn't sure how she felt about being alone in the home, of coming home to an empty house night in and night out.

Her phone vibrated in her pocket.

Just next door. The text was from her sister.

Come on over. The mayor is here too.

Charlotte's being in the Treasure Chest wasn't unusual, but why did Camille need to go there? She grabbed a chalkboard sign plaque and wrote, *Back in 5—next door if needed,* in pink chalk.

Once outside, she almost ran into Samantha Hill.

"Camille, seems I'm catching you at a bad time." Samantha took a step back, giving her room.

The reporter held a notebook in her hand, purse slung over her shoulder with the straps of what looked like a camera hanging out.

"Sam, good to see you. What can I help you with?" Camille asked. It had been a few weeks since she'd seen the woman.

"I thought I'd see what new stock you have today, and...maybe ask you a few questions."

Camille glanced at the store next door and noticed her sister in the window, beckoning to her.

"Hmm. Come back after lunch and I'll have new flowers out; they just arrived."

Sam glanced over. "Great. How about I bring you some coffee at the same time? I'll only take up a few minutes of your time; I promise."

Camille smiled. She liked Sam. "Stay longer or I'll be offended."

"Deal." Sam waved and headed down the street.

"Are you coming?" Paige stepped outside of the Treasure Chest and held the door open.

"You know there're arrangements due soon, right?"

Her sister nodded and glanced at her watch. "I know; I'm sorry. I ran into the mayor while getting a coffee and she dragged me here to talk about an idea she had."

"I did not drag you." Charlotte shook her head. "I merely

suggested you walk with me so we could talk."

Paige turned to Camille and mouthed, *Dragged.*

Camille gave her a small smile, then turned to the mayor.

She was always a little jealous of how classy Charlotte made casual clothing look. In dark skinny jeans and a tunic, not only did the mayor look comfortable, but she dressed it up with a chain and earrings. If Camille were to wear the same outfit, she'd look fat. It wasn't fair.

Charlotte noticed the items in Camille's arms. "I hope those are for here."

Camille placed them down on the counter. "Sure are. They're from Stan, my delivery guy. I sell his wife's tea and soaps, and the rest come over."

"I love that you support this place like you do." Charlotte smiled and opened up a notebook. "It's one of the reasons I thought of this and wanted to talk with you."

Camille looked over at Paige, who shrugged.

"I think it will be a while before Julia comes back to the shop, but I don't want it to close, and while it's doing okay as it is, I think it could be doing better. So I'd like to propose an idea." She looked up from her notebook and paused.

"Am I going to like this?" Camille asked.

"I hope so." Charlotte folded her hands in front of her. "I was looking through old blueprints of some of these shops and noticed something I never thought of before." She moved over to where an old china cabinet sat. Julia had painted it baby blue, and it was full of homemade baskets and other items. "There should be a door behind this cabinet linking the two stores."

"Really?" Camille's brow knotted as she looked at the area and tried to think what was on the other side of the wall in her shop. Some shelving and a table...but no doorway.

"I bet it'd be there. Remember Dad did renovations when we were younger?" Paige mentioned.

Camille was surprised her sister remembered that.

"Would you be interested in taking a look?" Charlotte asked.

"Why?"

There was a calculating look in the mayor's eyes before she relaxed her hands and spread them wide.

"I thought we could reopen that doorway between the two stores, generate more flow," Charlotte explained.

"Have you spoken to Julia about this?" Camille asked. It didn't make sense to connect the Treasure Chest with the flower shop, unless...

"You're worried Julia's not coming back," Camille said, the pieces falling into place.

The look now in Charlotte's eyes was of sadness. "I'm not sure how long Julia will need before she feels comfortable enough to come back, and we need this store to be up and running full-time." She shrugged. "Right now we've been able to get enough people to open it on the weekends, but...it's not enough."

Camille sighed.

"So you basically want me looking after the store." The last thing she wanted was more responsibility.

"I spoke with Julia, and she's going to ask Kerry Hurst to come back and help take care of it."

That surprised Camille. Kerry Hurst was a local retiree who used to work full-time with Julia until a few years ago. Something had happened between the two women and Kerry quit. Nothing had been said, but the two rarely spoke to each other in public since then.

"Do you think she's going to say yes?" Camille asked.

"I'm hoping."

"So why reopen the door then?"

"I think it would be a good idea to help with the flow of customers, and would be a good support to both of you in case someone needs to run out for coffee or..."

Camille chuckled quietly. From what she was hearing, Charlotte was having a hard time coming up with a good enough excuse, other than needing Camille to help watch over the store as a backup.

"Actually." Paige stepped up. "I think it would be something worth thinking over. Maybe it's time to expand the store into something more than just creating floral arrangements for orders, and this might be the thing."

Camille turned and gave her sister the scissor action with her fingers, their signal to each other for when it was time to stop talking or to be quiet. There was no expanding. No joining of the two businesses. They would discuss this together, in private, and not in front of the mayor, who would see it as a possible yes.

"Wonderful."

Camille turned to see Charlotte beaming at her.

"We'll talk about it and get back to you." Camille used a lower tone, not wanting to give hope when there might be none.

As if she understood, Charlotte nodded, twisted her hands together, and then attempted a cheery smile. "Good, that's all I can ask for. If you have any questions, let me know."

"Great. I need to get back." Camille turned to her sister. "Samantha came by and wants to do coffee after lunch, and Stan left a larger than normal delivery."

"Just give me a few minutes and I'll be right there."

Camille caught the look between her sister and the mayor as she left.

She didn't like it. At all. What was going on?

She tried not to think about that look while she was organizing the flowers, or while she rearranged the buckets in the fridge, or when she filled out the display buckets for the front of the store. She also tried not to look at her watch or the clock and count the minutes until Paige returned.

So when it took her sister over an hour before she walked through the doorway, it wasn't like Camille was beyond irritated or anything.

"So glad you showed up," she muttered while hunched over an

arrangement for a couple staying at the Seaglass Bed and Breakfast, celebrating their anniversary.

"I said I'd do those." Paige pushed the baskets on the table out of the way and set a tray of iced coffees and two paper bags down.

"We're running out of time. You can work on the next order." She added another rose to the vase.

"I'm sorry, but you know what Charlotte is like. When I realized the time, I thought you might be hungry." She pointed to the food she'd brought.

Camille remained silent.

"You probably want to know what we were talking about, right?" Paige asked after a considerable amount of silence.

"I'm a little curious." She'd imagined a hundred and one possible scenarios during the past hour and had come to one conclusion.

When Paige had told her she wanted to move out, Camille assumed she meant after the summer was over. She'd housesit for now and then look.

But she had a feeling whatever timeline Camille had thought up, Paige had her own plans.

Paige grabbed a spray and added it to an arrangement. "Seems that summer family I've been housesitting for won't be coming this summer after all, and asked if I'd be willing to rent their place for a year."

Camille's heart sank at the words. She knew it.

"Are you?" she asked.

"I said yes." Paige gave a small smile. "I know it's earlier than expected, but..."

"But now's as good as time as any, right?" Camille responded with lackluster enthusiasm.

"You okay with that?" Paige tilted her head to the side. "If Mom and Dad were still alive, we'd both be out on our own, living our own lives, right? I know things are different, that our lives are different now, but..."

"But nothing. It's a great opportunity and I think you should take it."

Relief flooded Paige's face. "You mean that?"

Camille nodded.

They worked in silence for a bit before Paige turned to her.

"There's something I want to talk to you about." Paige said.

Camille's hand paused as she cut some length off a rose stem. "What's that?"

"I'm really enjoying the landscaping aspect, more than I'd expected." Paige's nose wrinkled. "Dad would roll in his grave hearing me say that. He used to tease me that I'd fall in love with the feel of dirt between my fingers sooner or later."

Camille smiled at the memory as well, then sobered. "I also remember you swearing you'd never get into the flower business."

Paige shrugged. "Life changes, and you either roll with it or get left behind, right?"

The bell over the door rang, cutting Camille off from responding.

Samantha walked in, coffees in hand. "Is this a bad time?"

Camille looked at her sister. "Not at all."

"It's a beautiful day out; why don't we take the coffees to the park?" She hesitated for a moment.

"You don't mind, do you?" Camille asked Paige. She looked at the orders they still had left but figured she'd be back in time to help finish with the last ones.

Paige shook her head, pulling a stool out from the worktable. "I'm not going anywhere." She winked. "I'll work on these orders so they're ready for delivery this afternoon."

"We'll talk more when I get back, okay?"

Camille couldn't even begin to describe how she was feeling right this moment. She understood her sister's need to move out; Paige was still in her twenties, after all. Camille didn't like the idea of being alone at home, but she'd get used to it if she had to.

"Ready?" Sam asked as she waited outside on the sidewalk. "I won't take up much of your time, because I know you're busy."

Camille shaded her eyes as she glanced around her. "It's a nice break. Some days I barely get time to sit outside and enjoy the sun."

"I can drag you away more often if you'd like." There was a hint of warmth in Samantha's tone that caught Camille's attention.

"You're staying at the Seaglass Bed and Breakfast, right?"

Sam nodded. "It's a beautiful house, and Shelley is the perfect host."

"Are you enjoying your time here? Will you be staying with us for much longer or…" She thought for sure Samantha would have left by now.

"I find I like being here." Sam glanced around the park where they'd sat down. "There's something about Stillwater that feels like home to me. I decided to take a leave of absence from work and picked up a few articles from Arnold."

Camille breathed in deep and took a sip of her coffee. "Is this about one of those articles, then?"

Sam nodded. "Have you seen any of them? I want to focus on the people who live here, the ones who are the heart of the town. There's been enough negative focus over the past few months."

"Who are you focused on right now?" Camille asked. She really liked the idea, and even had a few suggestions for people if Sam needed any.

"Grace Bryar, the kindergarten teacher. Do you know her?"

Camille smiled. "Grace is a sweetheart. Everyone loves her, and the kids think she's amazing. Do you know that every summer she holds special picnics for the kids not only coming into her class, but also those who just left it? She does a lot of volunteer work as well around town. Basically anything that involves children, she's there."

Sam's brow furrowed as she took notes. "I heard she used to basically run the teddy-bear picnics."

Camille nodded. "She does. She was the one who actually started them."

"Really? I wasn't aware of that. I assumed it was another program Mayor Charlotte started." Sam made some more notes.

They sat there on the bench for roughly thirty minutes. Camille didn't mind answering questions; she would just need to remember to tell Grace so she wasn't caught off guard. Sam asked a lot of questions about Sophie, about Grace's relationship with Katie, Sophie's mother, but her questions were never intrusive.

"I hope you don't mind, but I've got you and Paige on the list of people to write about," Sam mentioned as they walked back to the florist shop.

"You do?"

"Your names keep popping up; did you know that? Specifically from Shelley, who has told me stories about your parents."

Camille just shook her head. Shelley Peters and her mother had been close, so that didn't surprise her.

"If you want to write about my parents, that would be lovely. I'm not sure how interesting Paige and I would be, though." They arrived at the shop and Camille peeked in through the open door. Paige was on the phone and beckoned to her.

"Listen, if you have a night free, why don't you come over for dinner?" Camille offered. If Sam was staying for a while, she could probably use some friends, if she didn't have some already.

Sam's eyes lit up. "Really? I'd love that."

They shared contact info before Camille headed into the store and listened in on Paige's one-sided conversation.

"Doris, I'm not canceling your daughter's flower arrangement. She likes to send these to you." Paige rolled her eyes.

Camille smiled. She was glad Paige was dealing with this and not her. Doris loved having flowers delivered to her but would complain every month or so that Charlotte was spending too much money on them.

"If you don't accept them, then I'm going to give them to

Jacqueline Willard," Paige threatened.

Camille almost snorted. There was a mutual hatred between Doris and Jacqueline, and it didn't help that their rooms were next to each other at the retirement home.

Nasty, Camille mouthed to her sister.

"Thank you. See you soon. Don't forget to put the teakettle on." Paige hung up from her talk and burst out laughing.

"Remind me to stop putting roses in Doris's arrangements. She thinks they're too expensive." Paige went back to one of the arrangements she was working on, shaking her head as she did so.

Seeing her sister there, working, Camille felt her heart swell. Paige belonged here with her in this store. Camille went over and gave her sister a hug, just because she wanted to.

"Thank you," she said.

"For what?" Paige looked up at her questioningly.

"For being willing to roll with whatever life hands you." Camille reached for an order and read through it. There were three arrangements left to make for today's deliveries; if they worked together, they should be able to finish them on time.

"About that...how willing are you to roll?" Paige asked.

Camille gave her sister a sidelong glance. "What do you mean?"

"Meaning I think we need to talk about Still Bloomin and making some changes."

Excited chatter interrupted them as a mother with her two daughters entered the store. With a sigh, Camille stepped away from her sister to see whether she could offer some help.

When she glanced over her shoulder, she caught the worried frown on her sister's face. What more was she going to throw at her? Changes to their business? Like what? Downsizing? Branching off? Hiring more people? What was wrong with the status quo?

Camille hated changes, and Paige was just throwing too many at her at once.

9

GRACE

GRACE WOKE up with a splitting headache.

"There's aspirin and water on your nightstand," John said softly.

Grace slowly sat up and reached for the glass of water, sipping it slowly before she took the two pills John had set down for her.

"Thank you," she whispered. She looked up and saw him sitting in her comfy corner chair, his legs crossed with a magazine on his lap.

"Have you been awake long?" she asked him.

"It's midmorning, Grace," John told her.

She groaned. "Where's Sophie?" She made as if to get up but John's words stopped her.

"Faith is taking care of her. They went out for a walk a little while ago."

She leaned back against her pillow instead and sighed with relief. Her head pounded, and she was filled with remorse for having drunk so much the night before.

"What time did we get home?" she asked John.

"I believe you slammed the front door around two in the morning."

"Slammed?"

He nodded.

"We walked home, right?" she asked hopefully. The last thing she wanted to hear was that they drove home after drinking wine.

"You walked. I headed over to Nathan's a little while ago and brought your car back. You handed me Sophie's car seat last night and asked me to put her to bed before you stumbled into our room and fell asleep."

"Sorry," Grace said. She couldn't believe she'd done that.

"Apparently we owe Nathan a few bottles of wine. You told me to make sure we replaced them before he came home. You had to drink the expensive stuff, didn't you?" John shook his head, but it was clear he was fairly amused.

She took that as a good sign.

"Was this before or after I handed you Sophie?" Things were fairly hazy in her mind. She closed her eyes and lightly rubbed her temple.

"After. You woke up when I was undressing you and told me you were sorry and that we should go away for a vacation, just the two of us, to Iceland."

She peered at him through one eye and frowned. "Iceland?"

He shrugged. "That's what *I* said."

"Why would I want to go to Iceland? Why couldn't I have said Hawaii or something?"

"Iceland would be cool, though, don't you think? I thought it was a good idea. At least you wanted to go somewhere with me, just the two of us." He leaned forward, elbows resting on his knees, and gave her a cute smile. "Or was that just the alcohol talking?"

"If I suggested Iceland, it's for sure the alcohol."

"I'm serious, Grace." John leaned forward, the magazine tossed to the side.

"I'm sorry," she said to him. "I'm really, really sorry. I...I shouldn't have gone to Nathan's and offered to stay there; I should have—"

"You should have stayed here and dealt with things. Running away never solves anything. Isn't that what you say to your students?"

She hung her head. "You're right. I guess I just thought it would be easier."

John stood and crossed the room. He sat down on the bed and reached for her hands.

"Easier than fighting for us? Than wanting to deal with whatever is going on between us?"

She stared at their joined hands, not saying a word. He was right. Absolutely right.

"You may want to give up, but I don't," he said.

"I don't," she said, shaking her head, then groaning at the same time.

"Do you love him?" John asked, his voice barely over a whisper.

"No." She squeezed his hand. "I meant what I said last night. I don't love him. I love you and only you. I'm sorry you thought that."

"Are you sure?"

"I promise. There is nothing between Nathan and me other than..." The words got stuck in her throat, and she had a hard time continuing.

"So there is something." John dropped his hands when she didn't answer.

Grace read the anguish in her husband's eyes and hated herself for it.

"No, no." She swallowed hard, closing her eyes, and prayed for strength.

"He hates me, John. He blames me for Katie's death—and he's right. He's absolutely right. It is my fault. The only thing between us is Sophie, and my need to help out. That's it. I promise." She begged him to understand, to believe her.

"He doesn't hate you." He cleared his throat before leaning forward, dropping his head between his shoulders, stooped and low.

What had she done to him? To them?

"He said as much last night. He blames me for Katie's death and wishes it had been me. If that's not hatred, I don't know what is."

"So you hate yourself, then; is that what I'm hearing?" John edged closer on the bed.

"I..." She didn't know how to answer. Did she hate herself? She blamed herself, knew it was her fault Katie was dead. Her own fault she miscarried. The stress of everything had been too much for her body. But did she hate herself?

"I don't hate you." John rubbed the back of his neck. "Your students don't hate you. Sophie doesn't hate you."

"Sophie's a baby."

John shrugged. "Babies are good judges of character. If I remember correctly, she doesn't like Arnold all that much. Every time she sees him she screams."

"That's not funny, John. Nor is it the same thing. Arnold scares even me." She gave a weak smile. "I don't hate myself; I just..."

"Blame yourself," he finished for her.

She nodded. "You must blame me too."

"No. I don't. But you can't keep letting that blame dictate things either." He stood up and moved so he could sit beside her. She snuggled in as he held her. "I'm not asking you to let go, or to forget and move on. I'm just... Just let me in. Let me help you with this. That's all I ask."

"What about Sophie?" She needed Katie's daughter to be part of her life. She needed it like she needed air to breathe.

"One day you're going to have to accept that you can't replace Katie in her life." John leaned his head against hers.

"I know," Grace agreed. "I don't want to replace her. I just..." She didn't know how to articulate the need within her properly.

"If Katie were still alive, you'd act like an aunt to her daughter, right? Offering to babysit every so often so she and Nathan could go out, buying her gifts, spoiling her rotten. Why can't you just do that now?"

"I am."

He shook his head. "No, sweetheart, you're not. You're taking the responsibility of raising her out of Nathan's hands and doing it for him. She needs her father, and I have a feeling he needs her too."

She swallowed hard. "You're asking me to step back, and I'm not sure I can do that."

Nothing was said for a moment until John leaned forward and looked her in the eye.

"So you're going to quit your job then?"

"No, why would I do that?" She loved her job. She had the career she'd always longed for. Her students were important to her, and she didn't want to give that up.

"Then what are you going to do come September? I'm sure the kids are already missing you. You don't go to the teddy-bear picnics; you're not at the beach; you're not spending time with your students like you normally do. By now you'd already have a *get-to-know-you* party for the kids coming into your class."

The weight of that settled on Grace's shoulders. Faith had basically said the same thing last night to her.

"If you're trying to make me feel guilty, you've done a great job." Grace bit her lip. Another failure to add to the list. She'd failed her class, her students....

"I'm not trying to make you feel guilty, Grace. Just to remind you that there's life to be lived outside of taking care of Sophie."

The sound of the front door closing and Sophie's cries caught Grace's attention.

"Just think about it, okay?" John asked. He relinquished his hold, as if knowing she'd want to get up now that Sophie was back.

Grace swung her legs over the side of the bed and paused.

Everything her husband had said made sense. Same with Faith. They weren't wrong. She had to learn-somehow-to stop blaming herself. She had to believe that it wasn't her fault Katie was dead. That it wasn't her fault she'd had a miscarriage. But it was a bitter pill to swallow.

"I'm going to need help," she said with her head hung low.

"Then I'm here."

"What about Faith?" she asked.

"Your sister is here too."

"I know that, but that's not what I meant."

"I know. Faith and I had a talk this morning over coffee. My jealousy of your relationship with her isn't fair. Not to you, nor to us. She's your sister. It's not fair of me to be jealous of your closeness. I just..." He glanced up to the ceiling. "I felt like I came second place in your heart, and I didn't like that."

"But, John, you don't. I don't know how many times I have to say it, but there's no contest between my love for you and my love for my sister."

"I know. Guess I've got stuff to deal with too." He leaned into her shoulder. "I love you, Grace Bryar. More than life itself. I don't know what I would do without you in my life; you know that, right?" He leaned his forehead against hers and stared deep into her eyes.

"I love you too, John Bryar," Grace whispered back.

10

CAMILLE

CAMILLE PLAYED with her napkin while waiting for Paige to show up for dinner at Gina's.

The moment she'd returned to the shop, they'd gotten swamped and barely had time to talk about Paige's ideas.

"Is Paige closing up the shop or finishing a job?" Gina refilled her glass of water.

"Closing up shop." Camille glanced at the time on her phone. Paige was fifteen minutes late.

"How about I bring you out some fresh bread and garlic butter?" Gina asked.

Camille's stomach grumbled.

"I'll take that as a yes." Gina laughed. She squeezed Camille's shoulder before heading back into the kitchen.

Camille looked around the café. The tables were starting to fill up with families, and she waved hello to many of the people she knew.

Paige finally joined her, sliding into the seat across from her, hanging her purse on the edge of her chair.

"Sorry that took so long. Just after you left a customer knocked at the front door. He must have seen the lights on."

"What did he need?"

The corners of Paige's lips lifted. "He lost his wedding ring on the beach."

Camille chuckled softly. "How many times have we heard that? Or lost in the water while swimming, or..." She shook her head as she thought about the multiple excuses they'd heard over the years when men showed up last-minute looking for flowers, thinking a bouquet would bring a measure of forgiveness.

"Thanks for your help this afternoon with the arrangements. I can't believe how busy it got with walk-in orders."

"That's what I'm there for, you know. To help. Sometimes I get so caught up working on other people's yards that I forget you need me in the store, so I'm apologizing for that. It wasn't on purpose, but it just..."

Tears formed in Paige's eyes as she struggled to finish. "I hate crying." She grabbed a napkin off the table, dabbing the tears away while her smile faltered.

"I know you think I spend too much time up at the golf course, and I probably do." Paige inhaled slowly. "You were right when you said I've been slacking, that I've paid more attention to the gardens at the golf course than anything else. I know it's silly, that there really wasn't anything between Ethan and me, at least not yet, but there could have been, you know?"

"I know."

"Sometimes I think that in all of this, he's often overlooked. I mean, compared to Katie and the kids." She stared past Camille's shoulder and shook her head. "No one seems to remember that Ethan was killed. So I thought..." She stopped, but Camille knew what she'd wanted to say.

"By keeping his gardens alive, you were keeping his memory alive."

Paige nodded.

"It probably helps that you prefer to be outside rather than stuck in the store, too," Camille said.

"I do, but that's no excuse. You need more help, and it's not fair of me to not be there."

Gina interrupted them by setting a basket of baked bread on the table.

"Fresh out of the oven. Now, have you had time to look over the menu, Paige, or would you like to go with the house special?" Gina pointed to the chalkboard on the wall.

Tonight's special was chicken Parmesan with browned-butter pasta. Camille placed her order and then asked for an extra take-out container. She loved Gina's food, and this saved her from cooking dinner tomorrow night.

"You know I can't pass up your pasta, and the chicken sounds delicious." Paige reached for a piece of bread. "I'm starving, so really, anything you offer would be good."

Gina patted Paige on the cheek. "You're such a good girl. Why don't we make a deal? You help me with my garden out front and I'll put aside a fresh meal for you once a week. We all know about your cooking skills, and you won't be having your sister take care of you soon, from what I hear."

Paige glanced from Gina to Camille and back to Gina. "When did you hear this?"

Gina shrugged. "Word spreads like wildfire here; you know that."

"What kind of help do you need with the garden, Gina? It looks fine to me."

Camille smiled as Gina explained that she was getting old, her back wasn't what it used to be, and she couldn't be bothered with the weeds anymore.

"This sounds like a deal made in heaven. Why don't I come by tomorrow and we can go over a schedule?"

After Gina had left, Paige leaned back in her seat. "This seems like the perfect time for me to bring up what I was trying to say earlier this afternoon," she said.

Camille studied her sister, not missing the look of excitement building in her face. Her smile was wide, her eyes bright as the words burst out of her.

"Since Mom and Dad died, we've done our best to keep their dream alive." Paige grabbed Camille's hand. "I think it's time that we change the focus from them to us. Our dreams, our goals…our lives. I know you love the flower shop, creating arrangements and chatting with people as they walk down the street. But I…" The smile on Paige's face grew. "I love to be working outside, in the gardens." She drew in a deep breath.

"Where are you going with this?" Camille asked.

"What do you think about creating a division, expanding our company with the landscaping? Make it official, rather than just a side gig?" Paige asked.

For a moment Camille said nothing, just sat there as if in shock. This was not what she'd been expecting at all. Expand the company?

"I'm serious," Paige insisted.

"I can tell…" Camille's eyes watered. "I think–"

"As the landscaping grows, we'll be able to hire someone to help in the store, giving you a break. With the additional income, you can go on your trip with Anne Marie and—"

Camille stopped her. "You've already sold me. We should probably look to hiring seasonal help anyway so we both don't get too stretched." Camille looked around and then leaned forward. "As long as you don't make too many of these special deals like you are with Gina," she said quietly.

Paige's face flushed. "I don't have to take the food. I'll manage on my own."

As if on cue, Gina appeared with plates of chicken Parmesan. "Honey, we all know how well you can manage. How many pots of water have you burned?"

Paige attempted to frown. "Hey, now. You promised not to bring that up. Seriously, I can manage. There's such a thing as TV dinners and ready-made meals."

"Take the deal with Gina. She'll give us free advertising, won't you?" Camille winked at Gina, who winked back.

"I sure will. Once you get a sign made, you can put it out in the garden, and even leave some flyers up by the register." She pointed to the food. "Now, eat up and enjoy."

After enjoying a few bites of her meal, Paige put her fork down on her plate. "Are you sure?" she asked.

"One hundred percent. We need to make this work for us in a way that will mean something. And while I'm not all that thrilled about you moving out, I get it."

"There is a benefit, you know. Now you can turn my bedroom into that office you've always wanted."

Camille thought about that for a moment. As far as she was concerned, her sister could take forever to move her things out of the house.

"Guess that means you need to hurry up and get your stuff out of there." She lowered her gaze. She wasn't sure how long she could keep the smile there.

"This is hard for you, isn't it?" Paige asked.

Camille shrugged.

"But you agree that it's time, right?" Paige pushed.

Camille sighed and put her fork down. "You know how well I react to change."

"Cam..." Paige pleaded.

"Having the cottage to myself might be nice. Especially if it means I get an office." She actually really liked that idea.

It was the look on Paige's face that did it for Camille: The tears came after she saw a flicker of happiness and contentment.

"You are not allowed to cry," Paige told her.

"Too late." Camille laughed while dabbing her eyes with her napkin. "Promise me one thing?"

"What's that?" Paige said.

"That we'll put aside one night a week for us? We'll do dinner and talk—about the business or about our lives, anything. Okay?"

"I'm only down the road, silly, but of course. How about we save Sundays for our time together? You can cook me dinner, I can bring dessert, and we can do some gardening together in the backyard."

Camille nodded. That would work. Sundays were always family days when their parents were alive. They would go to church together and then either play games back at home or go on a road trip. It would be nice to bring back that tradition.

"Now, about this idea. Can we talk about names?" Paige said.

"How about Bloomin Landscapes?"

"Oh, I like that. Look at you, using that marketing degree of yours," Paige teased. "It totally works with the family name too."

Camille breathed in deep, filling her soul with happiness. She liked the idea of changing the focus in her life, of rediscovering her dreams and having new goals. There were a lot of changes coming their way, it seemed, but Camille would just have to learn to *roll* with it.

How hard could it be, after all?

11

GRACE

"So it's official." Faith raised her phone and waved it. "I got an extension on my vacation time. Hope you don't mind having a houseguest for a little bit."

"Seriously?" Grace grabbed a top from the pile of laundered shirts and folded it. She smiled at her sister, glad that she was able to stay. She felt...complete with Faith here. Happier. Peaceful now that they were talking again. "How much time?"

"Till the end of summer." Faith flopped down on the bed. "Which means I can help you with the picnics for the kids, craft lessons, lying on the beach, eating ice cream, and getting ready for your first day of school."

"Teddy-bear picnics? You want to help with those?" Grace couldn't quite believe what she was hearing.

Faith shrugged. "Why not? It'll be fun, right?"

"I'll talk to the mayor and see if she still wants me to help, I guess." Grace knew she'd said she wanted help, that she needed to be pushed a little, but this felt like too much pushing all at once.

"We don't have to, if you don't want. I'm totally okay with lying on the beach and working on my tan. We could do some day trips down the coast too. My apartment in New York is a bit sparse and needs some coastal touches." Faith grabbed some laundry and began to help with the folding, and before Grace knew it they were finished.

"I can help with Sophie too, if you want," Faith mentioned.

Grace stilled.

"She certainly took a liking to you yesterday," Grace said, her voice weak. That was a good thing, Sophie taking to Faith. It meant things might not be so hard come September.

"You don't have to sound so surprised," Faith grumbled.

"No, it's probably good. She needs to get used to people other than me. You and John have a point."

"Good enough that you're going to start taking steps to..." Faith didn't finish her sentence, but she didn't need to.

"To let go of Sophie? Even though it feels like I'm letting her down?" She sat down on the bed and hung her hands between her legs. "Do I really have a choice?"

"You're not letting her down, Grace."

"Doesn't feel that way."

Nathan had come by late last night for Sophie, and when he asked whether she'd be around in case anything came up, as hard as it'd been, Grace said she had plans. Her hands had shaken as she'd closed the door behind Nathan, and her heart felt torn as she forced herself to walk away from Sophie's cries. But her husband was right: She wasn't Sophie's mom and she couldn't always be there to make Nathan's life easier.

"Lunch is ready." John appeared in the doorway. "Hope you guys are okay with burgers and salad."

"Fresh off the grill?" Faith jumped up from the bed. "I haven't had a good barbecued burger in a long time. Or steak, for that matter."

"Is that a dinner suggestion I'm hearing?" John asked.

"If you don't mind. I could run down to the store and pick up groceries," Faith offered.

"You're not paying for groceries—seriously, Faith." Grace said.

"Hey, if I'm staying for the rest of the month, I need to contribute in some way. Let me help with meals, okay?"

"Staying for a month?" John's brows rose.

"Will that be a problem?" Faith asked. She looked from Grace to John and back to Grace.

Grace shook her head. "Not a problem. Right, John?"

He nodded. "Not a problem at all, just caught me off guard." He breathed in nice and slow, and Grace realized right then just how much her husband was willing to bend and change for her. For them. For their marriage.

She needed to do the same.

"Faith mentioned wanting to help with the teddy-bear picnics." She hoped he understood what that meant, that he could read between the lines.

The smile on his face said it all. He'd understood.

"First she mentions steak and then this...could this day get any better?" He came over and wrapped his arms around her, holding her close. "If having your sister here makes things easier, then I'm okay with it," he whispered in her ear.

"Thank you," she said quietly, for his ears only.

The home phone rang and they all quieted. She hesitated for a moment, not sure whether she should answer it, but John had already picked it up.

"She's not available right now, Nathan. What can I help you with?" John braced one arm against the doorframe.

Different scenarios ran through her head: Something was wrong with Sophie; he couldn't get her to sleep; she was running a fever, wouldn't eat her food, or he couldn't get her to stop crying.

Grace opened her mouth to say something but he held up his hand as if to stop her.

She frowned.

"Yeah, I can hear her in the background. She doesn't sound happy. You should probably deal with that." There was a level of hostility to her husband's voice she didn't like hearing.

She tapped him on the arm but he ignored her.

"Dude, I feel for you. I really do. But this is your child. You need to learn how to comfort her before calling my wife for help."

Grace tapped his arm again, harder this time. She got what John was doing but it wasn't fair to Sophie. Her heart raced as she listened to the little one's cries in the background.

John looked at her finally but shook his head.

"No, you're right. I have no idea what it's like raising a child by myself and I hope never to find out. But this isn't my problem. I know it may sound harsh, but man up. Take responsibility instead of expecting my wife to always be there to help out. Have you thought about what will happen when Grace is back at work?"

Grace winced.

"No, I hear you. I do." John said, his voice now softer. "But when does it stop? Have you once thought about how it affects Grace? How hard this is for her?" John stared into her eyes as he spoke, and Grace realized he wasn't just speaking to Nathan, but to her as well.

She could hear Nathan talking but not the actual words. But whatever he said seemed to appease her husband.

"You need to make a decision, Nathan. Man to man, it's time you stepped up and took care of your family and stopped relying on others to do it for you."

If it wasn't for the fact John's voice was soft and warm, the words he was saying would come across as harsh and uncaring.

She really hoped Nathan wasn't taking it that way.

There was a loud screech and John pulled the phone from his ear. Sophie's screams were loud and clear, and Grace took the phone from his hand.

Enough was enough. Sophie was being placed in the middle of

this struggle for power between her husband and Nathan, and it wasn't fair.

He moved to stop her, but she stepped back before he could take the phone.

"Nathan, I'll be right over." She didn't wait for a reply before hanging up.

John's hand dropped. She read the hurt and disappointment on his face. "Grace, I thought we'd talked about this?"

Sophie's screams echoed in her ears, and she knew she couldn't leave the little one like that. Nathan was in over his head, and as much as she'd tried to be there to help him, she'd probably done more damage. Her being there to help whenever he needed it was like putting a Band-Aid over a wound that would never heal.

It was time to rip off the bandage. For both Nathan and herself.

It was time for her to stop using Sophie to cover her own pain of losing her baby.

"Trust me?" She placed a small kiss on his lips. "I love you and only you, John Bryar," she whispered. She stopped at the room where Sophie slept before leaving. For the past month or so Grace had been writing in a notebook, little pieces of advice, names of those who could help Nathan once she went back to work. Now was as good a time as any to give it to him.

Her sister waited for her, arms crossed over her chest.

"Don't do this."

"It's not what you think, Faith. I can't just leave Sophie like this. It's not fair to her." She needed her sister to understand that whatever changes Grace needed to make in her own heart, whatever issues she had...leaving Sophie to suffer wasn't fair.

"You have to stop running to him whenever he calls, Grace. You're not helping him, just enabling."

"I know. It's going to stop, I promise. I'm going to give him this." She held up the notebook. "It's a list of people he can call for help—people other than me." She waited for Faith to step out of the way.

"Why don't you come with me?" Grace called over her shoulder as she walked out of the house. With Faith there, she would have no excuse to stay and settle Sophie down, as she'd want to.

As they drove down the road, she looked back at her house and wondered why, if she was doing the right thing, it hurt so much.

Sophie was such a part of her life. How could she not be with the baby daily? Her arms would be empty. Her house silent. Sophie filled a hole in her heart Grace wasn't sure could ever be filled.

She knew this was what her sister wanted her to do. What John felt she needed to do...but what if they were wrong? In her head, the analytical side of her knew they weren't. But her heart? Oh, her heart hurt at the thought of not having Sophie in her life, of not seeing that little girl every day, or making her smile, hearing her laugh...it hurt more than she'd thought it would.

What if, by pulling away, she was hurting Sophie? Was it fair for the little girl to have the only two mothers she'd ever known ripped from her life?

Grace's heart almost stopped.

She'd just called herself Sophie's mother.

"Are you okay?" Faith reached for her hand. "Your fingers are freezing," she said as she rubbed them. "What's going through your mind?"

Grace pulled up to Nathan's house.

"I was just thinking of how unfair it is to rip the only two mothers Sophie has ever known away from her. She's too young for this kind of heartache." Grace swallowed past the lump in her throat.

"Oh, honey," Faith said.

"I love her, but what have I done? I'm not her mom; I can never be her mother, and I..." Tears streaked down her face as the burden of what she'd done hit her. She'd argued with John when he said she was trying to replace Katie. She'd convinced herself that she would never do that, that she *could* never do that, and yet...

"What you've done is exactly what Katie would have wanted you to do—love her daughter with all your heart. There's nothing wrong with that, Grace. Nothing," Faith handed her a tissue.

"So why does this feel so wrong?" Grace begged to know. Why was loving Sophie so wrong then?

"It's how Nathan depends on you that's the issue," Faith answered.

Grace looked toward the house and caught sight of Nathan standing on the porch with a clearly unhappy child in his arms. Sophie twisted and turned in his grasp as if trying to get out.

"It's going to kill me not to be there to help him with her; you know that," Grace whispered.

"That's not your responsibility. You've got to remember that. Love the little thing with all your heart, be there to help her grow into the young lady you know Katie would be proud of...but the raising part, that's up to her father."

She needed to find a balance; Grace realized that now. Not just a happy balance, but a healthy one too.

Grace's heart twisted at the sound of Sophie's cries as the infant's arms reached out for her.

"Why don't I try?" Faith reached out for Sophie instead, smiling at Nathan as she did so. "We got along pretty well yesterday; didn't we, sweetheart?" She jiggled her gently in her arms and walked toward the other end of the front porch.

Grace's arms felt empty, but she appreciated what her sister had just done.

"Thank you for coming, Grace. I know John didn't want you to, but..." Nathan trailed off. He stepped away from the door, beckoning her in, but Grace only shook her head and remained where she was.

"John was right, Nathan." Grace stared at her sister holding the now calmer child. "There is nothing I can do to replace Katie in your or Sophie's life, no matter how much I might want to. I love this little girl with all my heart, and I will always be here for her… but I can't keep doing this, Nathan. I'm sorry; I just can't."

Nathan frowned as confusion grew into realization. His shoulders buckled forward as if the heavy weight of Grace's words bore down on him.

She held out the notebook to him. "This is for you."

He took it from her hands and opened it. "What is it?" His brows knitted together as he read what she'd written inside of it.

"Suggestions for ways to help calm Sophie. Like how to put her to sleep, what she should be eating…all the important pieces of information I thought you would need from those parenting magazines Katie signed up for. At the back is also a list of people I think you should call." As she said the words, her soul grew calmer and she knew she was doing the right thing.

She would heal. They both would heal.

"You need someone to come in and clean the house. There are a few ladies in town who have a cleaning service. There is also a nanny service you might call—they can provide not just a nanny for Sophie but also a housekeeper. There's also a listing of teenagers in town who would love to babysit evenings and weekends—the ones I placed a star beside are my top picks. You also need to call Paige and ask her to come take care of Katie's gardens on a regular basis. Katie would be so embarrassed to see them this way." She rattled off all the information while keeping her focus on Sophie.

"Grace, I…I don't know what to say. This is all so overwhelming." Nathan staggered back, his whole demeanour screaming for her to help him.

Except she couldn't.

"At first I'm sure it will be, but it's time." She took Sophie from her sister's arms and held the little girl close. She breathed in Sophie's smell and kissed the top of her forehead softly. Sophie looked up at her with wide eyes, and it was all Grace could do not to break down in tears.

"I'll still be around, but not on a daily basis. I plan on being the best aunt your daughter will ever know, but..." She looked at her sister, who gave her a small nod, encouraging her to continue. "School will be starting soon, and I need to get ready for my classes. My sister is staying for the month to help me get ready as well."

"That's something you and Katie would do together," Nathan said softly.

Grace gave him a pained smile. "It's going to be different without Katie there." She kissed the top of Sophie's head. "I'm sorry, Nathan."

She was sorry for so many things, and she hoped one day he would be able to forgive her.

Reluctantly she handed Sophie back to Nathan and tried to ignore the way the little girl struggled to remain in her arms. "Be a good girl for Daddy, okay?" Grace reached for one of Sophie's hands and gave it a gentle squeeze.

"Why is she calmer when she's with you but like this"—he grappled with his daughter in his arms—"when she's with me?"

"I don't know what to tell you, Nathan, other than that you need to find a way to bond with her. I thought I was helping, but...apparently I was wrong." She reached for Faith's hand.

"Call those numbers in the book. Or your mom," Grace suggested. "There are a lot of people in town who would be more than happy to step up and help you if you just ask."

With one last look at the little girl who'd stolen her heart, Grace walked away. She'd have to be careful when she returned to not step back into the same pattern. It would be hard to not be with Sophie every day, to trust Nathan to be the father she knew he could be.

But she could love from a distance. She would work on repairing the rifts in her own marriage, and maybe...maybe one day having a child of their own.

But first she needed to heal and to grieve and figure out how to be the best kindergarten teacher Stillwater had ever had. She couldn't do that with a broken heart. Her kids deserved more. John deserved more.

She deserved more.

Thank you for reading Stillwater Tides. I hope you enjoyed it!

Turn the page for an excerpt from Stillwater Deep...

STILLWATER DEEP

STILLWATER

A Stillwater Bay Series

DEEP

NEW YORK TIMES BESTSELLING AUTHOR

STILLWATER DEEP

A STILLWATER BAY SERIES

There are so many people who helped in creating this story.

Thank you my amazing reader group - Steena's Secret Society! If it wasn't for your encouragement, your help...this story wouldn't be what it is today. Amy Coats, thank you for being the first to read and re-read this story, for being honest and for pushing me to do better.

For all the readers who kept asking me for the next story in Stillwater...this one is for you!

1

One month prior (from Stillwater Rising)

Charlotte's hands pummeled the punching bag with a steady rhythm. She pushed everything else out of her mind and concentrated only on her timing. Sweat dropped from her forehead, her chest hurt from the workout, and her knuckles cramped up from the constant impact, but she wasn't ready to give up, to give in.

"Will you talk to me, please?"

Jordan appeared in front of her, his hands on both sides of the bag, forcing her to stop. She bent down, her hands gripping her knees, and gulped in air.

"Go. Away," she managed to get out.

"No." His arms dropped from the bag, and he handed her a towel and her bottle of water. "I'm done with you avoiding me."

"Excuse me?" He did not just say that. He had no right. As far as she was concerned, she could and would avoid him as long as she needed to.

Two days ago he'd destroyed her world by confessing a secret she should have known from the beginning.

"We need to talk about this."

She wiped her face and took a long drink of her water before rolling her shoulders to work out the stiffness. She ignored him, as she'd done for the past two days, and walked past him and up the stairs.

She refilled her water bottle, cut a few slices of cheese, and went up to their bedroom, where she got ready for a cold shower. She knew Jordan had followed her. Knew he wanted to speak to her, needed her to say something to him. But she refused to.

She couldn't stomach the sight of him right now.

"I'm not going away, Charlotte." Jordan sat down in the armchair in the corner of the room and crossed his legs.

"What do you expect me to say, Jordan? That I forgive you? That I understand why you did what you did? That I find it perfectly okay that you would . . ." She couldn't say it. She just couldn't.

Everything made perfect sense now. Or not. God, no, nothing made sense anymore.

Two days ago when she'd found Jordan in Julia's backyard, she knew something was off. Why would her husband, the man who before the school shooting had happened, wanted nothing to do with Julia Berry, be in the woman's yard crying with her?

"No," Jordan said. "What I did wasn't okay, and I don't want your forgiveness. I don't deserve it."

"Then what is it you need?" Her body shook from unspent emotion.

When Jordan broke down after the ceremony where the glass heart memorial had been unveiled for all the victims of the Stillwater Bay school shooting, she'd told him that they'd deal with whatever had happened—together. But she hadn't expected this.

This, she didn't know how to fix.

"I don't know." His voice was full of remorse and rejection.

She turned her back on him and walked into their bathroom, locking the door behind her.

Leaning against the wall, she stared at herself in the mirror. She'd aged dramatically in the past two days. More wrinkles showed around her eyes and forehead, and the grey hairs in her hair had more than doubled.

Yesterday she'd locked herself in her office, and the only thing she'd done was look through old photos of her and Jordan, starting from when they first met. She wasn't sure what she'd expected to find in the images—a clue, maybe, to the double life her husband had led.

How could she *not* have realized there was something more between him and Julia? She's thought it odd that he never really seemed to warm up to her despite her and Julia being such good friends…she ignored the *elephant in the room*.

That was her mistake. She had to find a way to move past that, to focus on the bigger picture.

Her husband's cowardice.

He'd actually hid in a closet on the day Gabe Berry came into Stillwater Elementary with a gun.

What kind of man, principal, authority figure did that? When he'd first confessed to her, she'd thought she could handle it. Okay, so her husband was a coward and not the hero everyone made him out to be. She'd help him keep his secret. Right now the town didn't need to know he'd placed his own life ahead of his students'. That he'd hidden at the first sound of gunshots.

She tried very hard not to judge him for that.

But it was afterward—when they were at home, when he'd confessed his other deep, dark secret—that the world she'd known had been destroyed.

Gabe Berry, the sixteen-year-old who had shot and killed so many in May, had actually been Jordan's son. He'd been in a relationship with Julia before Charlotte met him, and he'd never told her. Never given the slightest hint about his and Julia's past together or that they'd had a child.

How did she fix this?

How could she face Julia again? One of her best friends—or so she'd thought. How could Charlotte look her in the eye and pretend everything was normal between them, when she knew about the secret between her and Jordan?

She couldn't pretend, and that was the issue.

Julia needed her right now more than ever before. She'd been labeled the mother of a monster and subjected to more hatred than a person should ever have to endure. Charlotte should be at her side, supporting her publicly, and yet...she couldn't.

Right now she couldn't distinguish between being a woman with a broken heart, and the mayor who should be strong.

When Charlotte emerged from the shower, Jordan was still there in the chair, waiting for her.

"All right, Jordan. You want to talk. You want me to open up and tell you how I'm feeling, is that right?" With her back turned toward him, she donned a sundress, pulled her hair into a ponytail, and took in a deep breath.

"Yes, that's what I want. That's what I need."

"Need?" She shook her head. "Right now your needs are the last thing on my mind."

She knew that from this moment on, things would never be the same between them again. Ever. She couldn't leave him. Not now. Not when her town was so fragile and needed her support and strength. But she didn't have any extra energy to put toward rebuilding her sham of a marriage, and to be honest, she wasn't sure she wanted to.

"Here's what I need. I need you to move out of our bedroom. Sleep in the guest bedroom downstairs or the one up here; I don't care. But you're not welcome here—in my room, in my bed. Not now. I'm not sure if you ever will be again."

Jordan cast his gaze downward but nodded.

"I also want you to start looking for a new position. Somewhere else. I don't care where. It can be in Seattle, Portland, or all the way across country. I. Don't. Care." She steeled her voice as he lifted his gaze and looked at her with shock. "Do you understand?"

God help him if he didn't.

"Why would you give up being mayor?"

She shook her head. She wasn't going to give up anything. Not for him.

Tears that gathered in his eyes as the understanding of what she meant hit him. "I can't do that, Charlotte. I can't."

She hardened her heart against him even more.

"You can and you will."

Two days ago Jordan had destroyed her world by not only admitting to his cowardice but also to the lie about Gabe that he'd lived for years.

The reason Gabriel Berry had gone into Stillwater Elementary with a gun was not because of some psychotic breakdown, but because he'd just found out who his father was.

2

One Month Later...(following *Stillwater Rising*)

Charlotte ran a hand through her messy hair and stared up at the popcorn ceiling above. She hated that ceiling. Late at night, the way the moon would shine and light up a section of her wall, it looked like tiny droplets of water just waiting to drown her in her sleep.

Every night since Jordan's big reveal, she'd stare at that moonlit sliver and dare the water to fall.

The fact that she believed it to be drops of water when she knew it was just her damn ceiling should bother her, but it didn't. She hadn't slept a whole night through since kicking Jordan out of her bed.

She stretched her arms out and rubbed the empty space beside her. She didn't like sleeping alone.

She missed her husband, plain and simple.

It was time to start focusing on the future. Her future. She'd said as much to Jordan last night. He'd asked her one simple question.

Did that future include him?

Rather than answer him then, she'd suggested they wait till today.

Over the past month, after making it clear to Jordan their marriage was over, she'd thought long and hard about what that would mean.

She'd tossed and turned all night, wrestling with her covers while mentally trying to come to a decision.

She'd made one.

"We keep talking about starting renovations but never get around to it. Maybe now we should?"

Jordan stood at the open door, jeans lying low around his waist and his hair dripping from his recent shower.

"Good morning." Him being here surprised her. For the past month, he'd waited till she came downstairs for coffee before coming up to their room. "Where's this coming from?"

"If we're going to talk about the future today, then I wanted to offer a suggestion." He took a step inside her room and sat on the corner of the bed and reached for her hand. "I know someone who could get started right away," Jordan offered. "I know you're worried about living in the house while it's being renovated, but I also know of a house that is empty that we could rent."

This was the Jordan she'd missed these past few months. The partner who took charge, who wanted to take care of her and one who worked with her, beside her, as a team.

Charlotte stared at his hand. She'd come so far in the past month. When he'd first confessed that he was Gabe's father, she couldn't stand the sight of him. She wanted him gone, out of her house and out of her life. But he'd begged her to not throw away what they had, to give them a second chance, that they were stronger together and the town needed them. As much as it tore at her inside to not throw him out right there and then...she'd listened.

How could she not?

He was right. They were stronger together. Or they had been, before she'd found out the truth beneath his lies.

Charlotte folded her arms over her lap. They hadn't discussed the changes they wanted to make to their home for months...not since before the school shooting. Their whole life had been on hold since that moment.

"Or not." He must have noticed her hesitation. "We can stay here and work on one project at a time if that's what you'd prefer." His shoulders straightened. "I'm not ready for a future without you in it, Charlotte. I love you and I will do whatever it takes to prove it."

She searched his eyes, looking for...what? More lies? More doubts and fears? There was nothing in his gaze other than complete honesty and love for her.

He came up here willing to do what it takes to make their marriage work, not realizing she wanted the same thing.

"One of the summer cottages?" Rather than focus on what he'd just said, she brought the conversation back to safer ground.

He shook his head, looking slightly off balance. "No." His gaze moved from her to the window. "During golf yesterday, Scott Umber offered up his house."

Her eyes lit up. "Are you serious?" She loved the Umber house. It was just outside the town border, but right on the shoreline, with a gorgeous wraparound balcony and the most beautiful library Charlotte had ever seen in a house. She'd once told Jordan she'd wished they could buy that home, despite knowing it would forever be out of their reach financially.

"They're headed to Europe for Christmas this year, so the house is ours as long as the renovations are finished before next summer." He rested his hand on her foot and squeezed slightly.

"We could, Charlie." Jordan leaned forward but he kept his hand on her skin. "We've talked about rebuilding this house, making it into the home of our dreams. It could be a fresh start for us." He swallowed hard. "For our marriage."

For their marriage. Charlotte bowed her head, twisting the wedding ring still on her finger.

She'd thought long and hard about their marriage for the past month, about what it would mean to end it—how it would feel, what it would cost her emotionally and how it would look to the town.

She didn't want to appear weak, and having Jordan at her side only contributed strength to the town…something Stillwater needed now more than ever.

She ignored that niggling thought that focusing on the town was a cop-out.

"A fresh start would be nice." The moment the words came out of her mouth, she knew it was true.

Jordan must have heard the truth in her voice. His shoulders dropped, his posture relaxed, and she could see the hope spark in his gaze.

"Do you mean it?"

Right now they were living in stasis, not really dealing with their past and definitely not moving forward. That wasn't what she wanted for her life, for them. She'd thought long and hard about what she did want—and despite everything that had happened, his secrets, his lies and deceit…she wanted Jordan. The life they had. They were stronger together and she needed that. Needed him.

"I want to mean it."

"But?" Jordan asked.

There were a lot of things she wanted to do but she'd learned early on that life never played fair. She should have known better when it came to her marriage…things were too good to be true.

"But," she breathed in deep, "let's take it one day at a time, okay?" Just because she'd made the decision to not end their marriage, didn't mean all the issues surrounding them vanished.

"Okay." He swallowed hard. "Okay, then. One day at a time." He nodded. "That is workable."

Workable. She was glad he used that word. Workable meant they were on the same page in regards to their marriage and what it would take to fix it.

"Why don't we go away this weekend?" He said.

Charlotte snorted. How did he get from taking it one day at a time to going away for a weekend?

"We haven't done that in a while," his words rushed out as if realizing how it came across, "and it would mean getting away from all the distractions of being here and figuring out how to focus on us again?"

Her first instinct was to say no, that she wasn't ready for what that meant, but if there was one thing Charlotte wasn't, it was a coward. Her gaze slid away from Jordan's at that thought.

She pushed it from her mind. She needed to. She had to focus on them, on today, now. One step at a time.

She didn't make half-assed decisions, so if she agreed to this, she needed to be sure. Offering a fresh start with Jordan meant starting over, moving past all the lies and deceits and moving forward to remain strong. Stronger.

"Okay." There. Decision made. "Why don't you have your shower and then figure out where while I take Buster for our morning walk."

"No requests?"

She shook her head. "Surprise me."

He jumped off the bed and pulled her alongside him, surprising her.

"Jordan!" She almost tripped over Buster, who'd jumped up from where he lay on the floor.

"Enjoy your walk. I've already got the best place for us to head toward in mind." The spark in his eyes was infectious.

"If it's that quaint little bed-and-breakfast by Samish Bay, I'm in. Now go on—scoot. You stink." She pushed him away from her, not kidding about the stench.

IT WAS EARLY ENOUGH that the beach was still fairly empty, and Buster loved nothing more than running after the stick. She liked it too. She wasn't a run-in-the-sand-while-sweat-dripped-down-her-skin type of person. She preferred taking her emotions out on her punching bag in a climate-controlled environment—mainly her basement—rather than dying of heat and having everyone see her sweating like a pig. But walking along the beach, listening to the waves lap along the shoreline…that she would enjoy for the rest of her life.

Her phone went off and Charlotte immediately hit the dismiss button before turning off the volume. It was her mom…and her mom was the last person she really wanted to speak to at the moment.

She'd just turned to close the gate separating her backyard from the public beach when she heard her name called out.

She should have gotten up earlier to go for her walk. Forcing a smile onto her face, Charlotte gave a little wave to the one person she particularly didn't want to bump into right now.

Samantha Hill, the UCN journalist from Seattle who had shown up in town to cover the school shooting and never left.

"Hey, Buster." Sam squatted down to pet the attention-loving dog before jumping back up and flashing Charlotte a bright smile.

Charlotte knew that smile.

"Why do I get the feeling you want something from me?" She knew exactly what the request would be…a one-on-one sit-down with her and Jordan.

"Probably because I've sent you numerous voice mails, emails, and texts asking." Sam gave her a look Charlotte knew all too well. She'd seen it a few times over glasses of wine and early-morning coffees. It was a look that said, *I always get the answers I'm looking for.*

Once things had started to quiet after the school shooting, Sam had decided to stay on in Stillwater Bay, renting a room from Shelley Peterson, who ran the Seaglass Bed-and-Breakfast. She worked on a few feature articles for their local town paper—articles that focused on the members of their community who'd impacted people's lives during the nightmare they'd all experienced. The goal was to focus on the good, not the bad—and not just on the lives lost, but on those who were still here, still hoping and believing that love could conquer all evil.

Charlotte really hadn't anticipated both her and Jordan being the focus of one of those articles, however.

"Right now there are more people you could surely focus on, right? Besides...weeks before the school opens is really not the ideal time for Jordan or me to sit down with you." She half turned to stare out over the beach, which was starting to fill with people walking along the shoreline. A beach full of people she'd worked so hard to protect and to help heal. She wasn't about to let a newspaper article destroy all that.

"I'd prefer we waited till afterward." She'd prefer they waited forever, to be honest.

At Sam's raised brows, Charlotte thought using her mayoral voice had gotten the point across—until she caught the slight shake of the reporter's head.

"Before the school reopens is the perfect time, actually, to have your joint article be printed," Sam argued.

The woman wasn't going to stand down, was she?

Charlotte rolled her eyes. She should have known better; this was a journalist she was talking to.

"I'm not going to stop asking." Sam gave her a saucy wink before picking up a stray stick and throwing it off toward the water for Buster to chase.

Charlotte sighed. "I'll need to talk to Jordan. He's not really... one to brag about himself." She now understood his reluctance, feeling it herself as she flamed the belief for his lie.

"Great. Sheila penciled me into your schedule for Monday. I thought we could do lunch?"

Charlotte pulled her phone out from her pocket and scrolled

through her calendar. "She did, did she?" She'd have to talk with her assistant.

"See if it works with Jordan; if not, we'll reschedule." Sam took the stick that Buster carried and handed it to her.

No longer in the mood for a walk, Charlotte tossed the stick over the hedge toward her backyard.

"Why don't I get back to you." She reopened the gate for Buster to go through. "Enjoy the rest of your run."

Sam reached out with a light touch to Charlotte's arm. "I'm sorry, Charlotte. You were out here for a nice morning walk and I disturbed that."

"It's…fine. I need to get going anyways." She gazed out over the beach and sighed.

"Busy day?" Sam asked.

"Just heading out of town for the weekend. A little R&R, you know?"

"Wow." Sam stepped back, arms folded and a wide smile on her face. "I don't think you've left town since May, have you? I'm impressed. Good for you guys; you probably need some time away, just the two of you. Your marriage has probably been the last thing on your list, I'm sure."

Charlotte forced a smile to her face. It was so easy for everyone else to have an opinion on what didn't concern them.

"Oh, I'm sorry." Sam covered her mouth with her hand, her eyes wide with apology. "I just overstepped. Damn. I do that a lot."

"Honestly, Samantha, I expect it from you. I don't think we've had a conversation since you've arrived where you haven't tried to step over that line." Charlotte shook her head, and this time the smile was real. "I'll talk to Jordan. Maybe we"—she gestured to Sam and then at herself—"can catch up on how things are going at the paper and what your plans are for the fall early next week, okay?"

"And confirm the date of the sit-down with you and Jordan?"

Like a dog with a stick…

"Fine, Sam. Fine."

Sam beamed a huge smile at her. "Have a great weekend, Mayor." She gave a wink before turning away.

Charlotte shook her head and followed Buster back into her backyard. She muttered a few choice words beneath her breath about nosy journalists before she walked into the house to find Jordan standing by the kitchen counter with his phone plastered to his ear.

"Great, thanks! We'll see you soon." Jordan gave her the thumbs-up as he hung up the phone. "You should hurry and pack," he said as he handed her a cup of fresh iced tea. "I've got Buster's things ready and our weekend is all taken care of."

"Whoa. Right now? Jordan, I can't leave that fast! I need to get in touch with Sheila and move some things around-" she stopped at the frown on his face.

"It's the weekend, Charlotte. Sheila is off-limits, remember? She needs a break too. And yes, right now. You can send all the emails and text messages you need to re-arrange your schedule when we're in the car."

Charlotte took in Jordan's damp hair and his relaxed stance. He obviously was looking forward to their weekend away, since he'd rushed to get ready.

"Fine." She tilted her head back and stared upwards, mentally counting until she didn't feel so flustered. He was right. She'd been the one to suggest Sheila be off-limits to her on the weekends and it wasn't like any of her coffee dates or other meetings were crucial. Everything could wait till Monday...

"Let me go throw a few things in my bag." She drank the tea and set the cup down in the sink. "I guess it was a good thing I'd cut my walk short."

"You didn't seem to get far," Jordan said. "Was that Samantha you were talking to?"

Charlotte gave a quick look over her shoulder outside. He must have caught them talking when she'd opened the gate.

She contemplated not saying anything—just ignoring the whole situation and making up a lie to Sam about how there was no room in their schedule to sit down, and keep that lie going as long as she could.

But knowing Sam, she would see right through her and contact Jordan directly. She'd gone so far as to get Sheila involved already because Sam knew Charlotte would continue to ignore her request.

"You know those articles Samantha is writing for the paper? Well..." Charlotte drummed her fingers on the counter. "She wants to write one on us, as a power team holding this town together since the shooting."

"And..." By the look on her husband's face, he understood how much of a mistake this would be. Guilt, shame, grief...they were etched on his face.

"And"—she let out a long breath—"I don't think that would be very wise, all things considered."

A wave of obvious relief washed over Jordan's features.

"The last thing we need right now is someone digging through your closet and figuring out the inconsistencies of your story. This town is just starting to heal, Jordan. They don't need to know about your connection to Gabe and the reason he brought that gun into the school."

Jordan's head dropped, shoulders stooped at her words.

"Maybe that's not such a bad thing," he said. "Maybe coming clean, being honest would be better than any false facade we try to maintain?"

"Excuse me?" How could he honestly think this would be a good thing?

"No." Charlotte reached out for him and took his hands, holding them tightly within her own. "No, Jordan. No one can know. Ever. Your confessing the truth only helps you...not those your secret destroyed."

Some secrets were better left unspoken.

"What kind of man am I if I don't accept responsibility for my actions?" He pulled his hands from hers and turned.

"A man who *is* accepting his responsibility." She placed her hand on his back. She pushed the panic as far down as she could in order to keep her voice steady and firm. "A man who is putting the needs of others ahead of his own." She gripped his arm and pushed so he'd turn back around. She needed to look him in the eye, to see that he understood. "A man the town expects and believes you to be."

She needed him to believe her. To trust her. To trust in her. She was right; there was no other way to handle this, and he needed to realize that. Their town wasn't strong enough for the truth, for him to bare his soul. She wasn't ready for it, for how it would damage them...no, that didn't matter. It was about the town, not them, not her.

He looked deep into her eyes, his own full of anguish, and she knew how hard this was for him.

"What about you?" he asked. "What kind of man do you believe me to be? I've screwed up so much, Charlotte." His fingers ran through his hair, messing it up. "Will you ever be able to forgive me?"

And there was the question of the hour.

"Forgiveness is a choice, Jordan," she said quietly.

He didn't blink, didn't move a muscle while he waited for her to answer his question.

There was a lot she wanted to say. A lot she needed to say but never would. Like how she wasn't sure she'd ever be able to respect him again even though she knew she'd need to. Like the waves of anger that would hit her when she'd least expect it, anger at him for what he did to Julia, to his son, to her.

But she couldn't think about herself right now and her own feelings. She had to put that aside and focus on the greater good... what her town needed.

"We can't let our past mistakes define who we are—no matter what those mistakes may be."

Instead of focusing on how she felt, she thought of their life together, of what he meant to her, and she poured those memories, those feelings into what she said next.

"I believe you to be the man who will stand beside me as we do what's best for our town. I believe you to be the man who will place us and our marriage first. I believe you"—she gave him a soft smile—"to be the man I need in my life."

A look of instant relief flooded Jordan's face as he pulled her into his arms and pressed her close. Eventually she rested her head on his chest.

"Trust me, okay?" she asked. "We will get through this." As long as they stayed strong together, maintained their solidarity, things would be fine.

They had to be.

3

"IT'S SO SAD, what happened in your town. I pray for you all every night." Mrs. Grimshaw reached for Charlotte's hand and squeezed.

"Thank you. We can feel those prayers, for sure." Charlotte gave the elderly woman a smile before she glanced down the beach, praying for Jordan to appear.

He'd left an hour ago to take Buster on a walk before they headed home from their weekend getaway.

"It's just so tragic. You never think something like that could happen in your own backyard, you know?" Mrs. Grimshaw continued without missing a beat. "I wasn't sure if we'd be seeing you this summer or not, all things considered." Mrs. Grimshaw reached for a basket she'd set to the side. "When Mr. Grimshaw told me you were finally coming, I knew I had to rush back from Seattle to see you. I'm so glad you hadn't left yet."

"It's been so nice to see you as well," Charlotte infused a smile into her voice. There'd been nothing nice about this trip. It'd been a mistake from the moment they'd arrived.

"Where is that handsome husband of yours? When we heard the news," Mrs. Grimshaw clutched one hand to her chest, "our hearts were just torn, you know? We sat in front of our television to make sure we didn't miss anything. We were so proud of you both, we even told our guests that have come all summer that you are our regulars. I'm so glad you were able to come this summer." She held the basket out to Charlotte.

"You didn't need to get us anything." Charlotte murmured as she looked through the assortment of jellies and crackers, crocheted clothes, some candles and bath salts.

"I just wanted you to know you're not alone." Mrs. Grimshaw pulled Charlotte into a tight hug, the basket digging into her hip.

Charlotte glanced down the beach again.

"I can't tell you how much we appreciate this. Thank you." She opened one of the doors to her vehicle and set the basket inside, on top of her weekend bag. Charlotte was in a rush to leave. She wanted to head home. Soak in her tub, drink some wine and be alone.

What was supposed to have been a relaxing weekend away turned out to be full of stress and arguments. The Grimshaws had hearts of gold but from the moment they'd arrived, there hadn't been one moment of peace. Word had spread that they'd arrived at the guest house and whether they sat on their porch sipping coffee or were walking Buster along the beach, someone would arrive with plates of fresh baked goods and want to chat.

Inevitably it was always about the school shooting.

So much for getting away from it all.

"I sure hope you didn't mind all the people who came by to see you and Jordan. I know you probably hoped for some peace and quiet but...well, like I said, it's not every day something so tragic happens in your own backyard." Mrs. Grimshaw fiddled with her hands and didn't quite meet Charlotte's gaze.

Charlotte kept the smile on her face and breathed a sigh of relief as Jordan appeared. Finally.

"Of course not. Thank you so much squeezing us in last minute." Charlotte had been surprised when Jordan at first mentioned they had a cottage available. It broke her heart to realize visitors along the coast had been sparse following the events in their town.

"How could we not? This might be our last summer out here. Mr. Grimshaw wants to sell the place before next season and move into the city. Of course I don't mind...with five grand-babies now, it would be nice to be close by, you know?"

Charlotte caught the unsettled fear in the woman's gaze as she glanced towards her husband who stood on the porch, leaning heavily on his cane as he stood on the porch.

The news didn't surprise Charlotte. The Grimshaws were getting up in age and probably couldn't manage the bed and breakfast for too much longer.

"Sorry we took so long." Jordan said as he stood at Charlotte's side. "Buster didn't want to get out of the water." He opened the trunk of their vehicle for Buster to jump up. "We should probably get going. Tyler called and is coming over tonight to discuss some staffing issues for the school."

Charlotte narrowed her gaze at him. "What happened to being phone free all weekend?" Both of their phones, or so she'd thought, were locked in the glove compartment of the vehicle.

"Oops." He gave a sheepish shrug, but from the look on his face, he really didn't care.

That was fine. Two could play that game.

After saying goodbye to their hosts, Charlotte pulled out her phone and rather than talk with Jordan during the drive home, she spent time answering text messages and emails.

A good thirty minutes into their drive, Jordan reached over and covered her phone with his hand.

"I'm sorry, okay? I didn't figure you'd mind since I was walking Buster alone. If you'd been with me..." his voice trailed off, leaving the idea out there that if she'd joined him, he wouldn't have had his phone with him.

"I needed to pack things up and you were only supposed to be gone twenty minutes tops." She set her phone aside and crossed her arms over her chest, staring out the window.

That's what bothered her the most. That he'd been gone for so long, leaving her to deal with the Grimshaws on her own, especially after she'd told him she didn't want to be alone with them, again.

Charlotte was talked out. For someone so extroverted, this weekend exhausted her and she needed time away from being away.

It didn't help that the limited time her and Jordan had spent alone wasn't exactly what she'd call quality time.

"I'm sorry." Jordan repeated. "Tyler called and I lost track of time."

Funny, but he didn't sound all that sorry.

"So, Tyler is coming by the house then?" So much for her night of quiet.

"No. I'll meet him down at the pub." He looked over at her and frowned. "You can join us if you'd like?"

Like that was going to happen. Tyler was Jordan's friend. Not hers.

"Thanks but no thanks. My plans tonight consist of a hot bath, a new book and maybe drink a full bottle of wine. I'll try to salvage as much of this weekend as I can in a few hours."

"I'm sorry this weekend wasn't what we thought it would be." Jordan gripped the steering wheel with both hands and didn't look at her.

She tried to read him but he'd closed himself off from her. She didn't blame him.

They'd argued last night about his relationship with Julia. Charlotte had drank too many glasses of wine and started to ask the questions she'd bottled up for so long.

Jordan didn't have much to say and what little he did, Charlotte hadn't liked his answers.

"We probably should have waited." Charlotte thought back to the words he'd said to her last night.

No matter what I say, it will never be what you want to hear.

That wasn't true. She just wanted to understand, was that asking too much?

"We never would have taken the time, you know that." Jordan didn't release his grip on the wheel.

"If it's important enough, you make the time." Charlotte's mother used to always say that to her.

Jordan shook his head.

Charlotte leaned back in the seat and turned the volume of the radio up. If all they were going to do was argue, she'd rather not talk at all.

"You can't hold what happened seventeen years ago against me, Charlotte." Jordan turned the volume down, his shoulders set back.

She ran her fingers through the back of her hair, dislodging her ponytail in the process.

"I'm not holding it against you. I just need to understand how you could keep something like that a secret from me." Why didn't he understand that?

She thought she could handle knowing her husband and one of her best friends had been an item – no matter how brief. She thought she could. But she couldn't.

Not only that they'd been an item, but they had a child together. A child she'd never known about.

How could she let that go?

"I don't know how much more I can explain myself for you to understand. We dated only a few weeks. There was nothing to our relationship. Nothing to tell or explain. I didn't even recognize her when she first moved here. God," he rubbed the back of his neck, "that was a lifetime ago, Charlotte. I'm sorry. I didn't think a few weeks of my life with her was worth mentioning."

Charlotte's seatbelt cut into her side as she twisted in her seat. She clenched her fingers in suppressed anger.

"Nothing to explain? How about the fact you had a child with her? That you were a father to some little boy? It's one thing if you hadn't known about Gabriel..." she chocked on the words as they came out. Her heart raced with anger while she struggled to breath properly.

"I never wanted to be a father. Julia knew that. It was her choice to raise the boy alone. Why is her decision my fault? I gave her money, made sure she was taken care of as much as I could in the beginning. She was the one who didn't want my money or my help afterwards...so why am I paying the price now for her choice?" He pounded the steering wheel with his fist.

The level of his anger and obvious frustration startled her.

"It's one thing to not want to be a father. I get that, Jordan. We both agreed that children weren't a part of our lives. But it's another to ignore the boy after Julia moved here. That's what I'm struggling with. Not to mention the fact you both kept this from me." Her jaw clenched as she tore her gaze from her husband to the scenery that sped by.

"I wasn't keeping anything from you." Jordan breathed in deep and rolled his shoulders.

"You were. How can you deny that?" There was a dull throb of pain in her head. Charlotte scrambled through her purse for Tylenol and washed two pills down with a bottle of water.

"I'm sorry. I don't know what else to say."

Charlotte barely heard him, his voice was so low.

"I tried to respect Julia's decision. I waited to see if she'd say anything to you or if she'd talk to me about Gabriel. But she never did. So I never did." His tone was apologetic. Charlotte wondered if he truly was or if he was only telling her what he thought she wanted to hear?

"But you should have."

He nodded. "I should have."

A tear trickled down Jordan's face. He quickly wiped it away and put his sunglasses on. If he'd hoped to hide the tears from her, he was too late.

Charlotte reached out and entwined her fingers through his. His hold was stiff, unbending for a few moments until the tension in his hand released and his fingers curled around hers.

"I'm sorry." She said. As much as he said he never wanted to be a father, Charlotte couldn't help but wonder if deep down, he regretted making that choice.

"I'm sorry too. More than you could ever know." The words tore from his throat, confirming Charlotte's suspicions.

"We'll get through this, Jordan. We will." The need to reassure him was heavy on her heart. She didn't know what it would take for them to get past this but she was willing to try.

Her cell rang just then.

"If you want to answer that, it's okay." Jordan released her hand so she could pick up the phone.

Seeing that it was her mother, Charlotte thought about answering it. She thought about how the conversation would go and realized she didn't have the energy to deal with any crisis or requests her mom had for her tonight.

She hit the ignore button.

PURCHASE STILLWATER DEEP TO KEEP READING

WANT TO READ MORE?

Sign up for my newsletter to be the first to know when I have new releases coming out! Not just new releases but other fun things like secret postcards in the mail, contests, giveaways and more! Trust me...you want to sign up!

Newsletter Sign Up

Can I help you celebrate your birthday?
Sign up to receive a birthday postcard from me!
I also send Christmas cards too :)

PS...if you happened to have left a review for this story - thank you! Reviews help in more ways than you can imagine!

Happy Reading!

STILLWATER SHORES

STILLWATER

A Stillwater Bay Prequel

SHORES

STEENA HOLMES

NEW YORK TIMES BESTSELLING AUTHOR

STILLWATER SHORES

PREQUEL TO STILLWATER RISING
BOOK ONE

STEENA HOLMES

www.steenaholmes.com
www.facebook.com/steenaholmes.author
www.twitter.com/steenaholmes

ISBN: 978-0-9920555-5-4

ISBN: 978-0-9920555-5-4

A NOTE FROM STEENA

STILLWATER SHORES was once called BEFORE THE STORM.

The story is the same - the only thing that has changed is the cover and the title.

The reason for the changes is for branding purposes - the title fits better in with the rest of the series titles and the same with the cover - I felt it works better.

Thank you to the readers who would continue to ask me to rebrand the covers and this title specifically.

1

CHARLOTTE STONE

Present Day: Friday, June 21

One by one, members of the small town of Stillwater Bay headed into the community church, their heads lowered, their hands clasped, their footsteps muted as they came together to say goodbye.

Charlotte Stone kept her head raised, her glance steady, her hands available to touch a shoulder or to give a hug when needed. She would stay strong for those who couldn't, and on a day like today, not many could.

How did you say goodbye to a child? What words could you say to someone who lost their son or daughter in a senseless act while the world looked on?

There were no words. No promises of a better day. No explanations of why God turned his eye when he should have been protecting with his hand and heart.

She kept her attention on the one journalist they'd allowed into the service. While Charlotte trusted Samantha Hill to respect the privacy of the families there today, she also knew the reporter had a job to do. Right now Samantha stood with Jennifer and Robert Crowne, and Charlotte felt a twinge of guilt knowing she was the reason they were speaking with Samantha.

There were twelve families grieving today. Twelve families who had lost a child or a spouse in the nightmare of the school shooting three weeks ago. Today was meant for the town to come together to honor those lives lost, to remember them and be there for the families It wasn't meant to be a day captured by the media.

And so, instead of all twelve families being forced to once again have a microphone in their faces or be seen on the news, only one family stood there. A few days ago, in her office at Town Hall, it had been Robert who offered himself up to speak when the idea had been suggested.

While Robert remained stoic in front of the microphone as Samantha asked him a question, Jenn stood there, dressed all in black, her hands clutching at the small purse in front of her body like a shield. Charlotte made her way down the stairs of the church and stood beside her, placing her hand on her friend's back to let her know she was there.

She wasn't even sure Jenn noticed.

Jenn held her body straight as a board as she stared out across the street to the town park. Her gaze, empty. Charlotte wondered if maybe she was on the medication her doctor had prescribed. Since her youngest son was shot dead, Jenn had retreated inside herself, unwilling—or maybe unable—to interact with anyone.

"Mr. Crowne, thank you for taking time to speak with me today. I have one final question for you, if I may?" Samantha hesitated and glanced at Charlotte, as if asking for permission. Charlotte looked to Jenn, and then to Robert and caught the tight lines around his mouth and the way he swallowed, as if holding back his emotions. Robert gave her a look along with a slight nod, as if to tell her he was okay.

"We need to head into the service, so please make it short." Charlotte took a step up and angled her body toward Samantha, hoping to act as a shield for Jenn.

Samantha nodded, glanced down at her notes, and looked back up, her head held high. From the way the woman squared her shoulders, as if finding the strength deep within to ask the question, Charlotte knew it wasn't going to be an easy one.

And that ticked her off. She'd specifically told Samantha to be gentle, not to prod too deeply today; otherwise she'd be banned along with all the other media snakes who were parked along Main Street hoping to catch a glimpse of the families as they entered or exited the church.

"Today is meant to be a day of remembrance, correct? A day for all the members of Stillwater Bay to come together to mourn the lives of those who were killed during the shooting at the school. And yet there is one person I haven't seen arrive, and I'm wondering . . ." Samantha paused, and Charlotte wasn't sure whether it was for effect or courage. "Do you think Julia Berry, the mother of the teen shooter, Gabriel Berry, will be here? And most important, would she be welcomed?"

Before Charlotte could step in, Jenn woke up from her daze, fury on her face, and she grabbed the microphone from Samantha's hand.

"We are here to mourn the loss of our children, *not* to focus on the one who took them away from us. How dare you even ask such a thing!"

Charlotte reached for the shaking microphone in Jenn's hand and handed it back to the reporter.

"That was uncalled for. If you have any more questions, you can wait until tomorrow and come by my office." She stared down at the woman, who at least had the decency to look ashamed. And so she should.

Charlotte waited while Robert led his wife up the stairs into the church, and then took a step into Samantha's personal space.

"I was very specific about the line drawn here today." She clenched her jaw and forced the smile to remain on her face. No need for everyone around them to know something had just happened.

"And I didn't cross it. As agreed, I spoke only with Robert and left the other families alone." Samantha stood her ground, lifting her chin.

For that, Charlotte was impressed. Most people would have backed down already.

"No, but you asked a question you had no right to bring up. Not to them."

Samantha nodded. "You're right. But you keep saying this is a tight-knit community, going so far as to call it a family. If Julia Berry is part of this family, then shouldn't she also be welcomed today? From what I've heard, she's an integral part of this town. Or am I wrong?"

Charlotte sighed. How was she to answer that? Until the day Julia's son walked into the public school and killed ten students and two teachers, Julia had been one of the strong foundations of the community, a person others could count on—and one of Charlotte's good friends.

She was still Charlotte's friend. That would never change.

"It was Julia's choice not to come today. She didn't want to add more distress to the families, and I think she made the right decision."

"So she's not ostracized then?"

What a word to use. Unfortunately, it was probably the right one too, as much as it hurt to admit that.

"The decision was hers."

"So you're saying that if Julia Berry were here today, she would be welcomed inside the church and be allowed to mourn the loss of her son's life alongside his victims?" Samantha asked.

"What do you want me to say, Samantha?" Charlotte clenched her fists in anger.

"Sometimes"—Samantha's voice softened, reminding Charlotte why she liked her so much: because she wasn't afraid to show her heart—"we have to face the truth, even when it hurts."

Charlotte stood there for a few moments, struggling to think of what to say and how to say it. The truth was gritty and ugly and a huge mess. But did that need to be made public? There were good people here in Stillwater Bay. Good people who didn't deserve to have their lives ripped apart like they had been for the past few weeks, thanks to a senseless and unanswerable crime.

"Charlotte?"

She turned to find her husband, Jordan, holding the door open at the top of the stairs.

"You need to come in now."

She gave him a smile in thanks and saw something in his gaze that gave her the words to say to Samantha.

"The truth is that we are a town full of grieving families and it's going to take time to heal. But we will heal, and we'll do it together. That's what makes Stillwater Bay so unique—because we're not just a community; we are a family." With that, she turned and walked up the stairs to meet her husband at the door.

They were a family. She believed that with all her heart. It was the cornerstone of the strength of their community, why they continually rose above anything that came their way—because they took care of one another.

And yet she'd be blind not to admit that there were cracks in that foundation, and she was more than just a little worried that those cracks would grow until everything around them came crumbling down.

CHARLOTTE PAUSED for a moment before she entered the church

sanctuary, needing to take everything in. All the seats were full and there were even some people who stood off to the side.

The church was brightly lit; soft music was being played on the piano at the front, where Scott Helman and another pastor stood. Scott had introduced them earlier, but for the life of her, Charlotte couldn't remember his name—until it hit her: Mark. Reverend Mark Giffin, an old mentor from Scott's days at seminary. He'd come today to help support Scott and lead the service, allowing Scott to sit with his family and actually take time to mourn, or at least try.

At the front were framed pictures of the victims, along with a beautiful array of wreaths and objects that represented them.

She saw Bobby's photo first as she walked up, Jenn's son, and tears welled up in her eyes. There was a small bouquet of flowers by his picture, but there was also a large stand full of miniature cars and trucks. She smiled through her tears; that boy sure did love his toys. Jenn had bins all over the house full of LEGOs and small vehicles, and whenever Charlotte came over for coffee, she'd inadvertently step on one or two while she was there.

The last time she'd been there, she'd broken a hinge off the door of one of the cars. She reached inside her purse and pulled out the replacement she'd bought for Bobby but never given him. She swallowed hard as she placed it down on the stand. She couldn't look at Jenn, not yet; otherwise she wouldn't be able to contain the sobs that wanted to come out.

Crying was out of the question right now. She needed to be strong, to be sympathetic but a shoulder for others if they needed her. She could and would cry later—in the shower, as she'd been doing off and on for the past three weeks.

Next to Bobby's picture was Wes's, Lacie's beautiful boy. His smile always lit up the room, and he was so kind and gentle. What would Lacie do without him now? What would Liam, their other son, who had Down syndrome, do without Wesley there to help calm him down?

Then there was a photo of Katie Hansen, the kindergarten teacher who was shot while protecting her students. Hers was a very sad story. She'd just given birth to a beautiful little girl and had been called in as a substitute for the day.

The other adult who died had been an innocent bystander, someone who just happened to be in the wrong place at the wrong time. Ethan Poole was basically a kid himself, and from what she'd heard, he'd been at the Golf and Country Club working when he'd received a call that his nephew had forgotten his backpack in his pickup truck. He'd been at the school only to drop it off when he'd been caught in the cross fire.

It was hard to see all the images, to see the youthful faces, their smiles that would never light up again.

Charlotte made her way to her seat beside Jordan and placed her purse in her lap. She looked at her husband, saw the grief-stricken look in his eyes, noticed the way his hands trembled and the curve of his shoulders and how he tried to hold back the tears. He should have seen the signs years ago. He was trained to, as the principal of a school, after all. Why hadn't he?

Charlotte knew Jordan had issues with Gabriel when he was in his school. He'd often come home at night and complain about the boy . . . but did he try to help him? Charlotte couldn't remember.

If he had, if he'd spent time with the boy and tried to understand him, maybe all of this—the heartache, the loss, the grief—maybe it wouldn't have happened.

Hours later, after the service, Charlotte told Jordan she'd see him at home later and walked down the street to where Julia lived.

Julia sat huddled on her couch, a blanket wrapped around her thin body. Her eyes were dry but sunken, and Charlotte had to open every available window to help breathe new air into the small home.

She'd picked up a small casserole she'd left in her vehicle earlier and brought with her, but when she walked into the kitchen, she realized she should have brought something else. The cupboard was full of sandwiches and salads, the table covered in muffins and biscuits, and when she went to place the small dish she'd brought with her, she realized both the fridge and freezer were full. This warmed Charlotte's heart, knowing there were still some members of their community who didn't view Julia as anything other than a grieving mother.

"Julia, have you eaten anything at all?"

She shook her head. "I'm not hungry."

"You need to eat."

Julia shrugged. "Could you take some of that food over to the church or the retirement home? I'm sure they could use it."

Charlotte sighed. It would only go to waste here, so yes, she'd take it, but . . .

"On one condition: You eat a plate I make you of something light. Okay?"

Julia looked at Charlotte for a moment without saying anything and then smiled. It was weak and small, but Charlotte would take it.

She fixed her a plate with a cucumber sandwich cut into four pieces and added some salad greens. She made a plate for herself so that Julia wouldn't be uncomfortable eating in front of her.

"How was the service?" Julia's voice cracked.

"It was nice." The word was inadequate, but then, how would you describe a memorial service for the victims to the mother of the boy responsible for their deaths?

The silence in the room was thick and tangible, and Charlotte was at a loss for words.

"I made the right decision not to go, didn't I?"

Charlotte nodded.

"Lacie told me I should have gone."

Charlotte opened her mouth and then closed it, shocked at the news. Why would Lacie do that? How could she? Julia's being there would have been like a . . . like a slap in the faces of all the families, even though she had every right to be there. What had Lacie been thinking?

Lacie was Julia's best friend; they were inseparable, and Charlotte couldn't imagine the pain that had torn them apart after Gabriel killed Lacie's son Wes. She wasn't sure how their friendship could survive, and wouldn't have thought Lacie would be talking to Julia just yet.

"Why?"

A sad smile settled onto Julia's face. "She said I was as much a victim as anyone else and grieving for my child too."

"Oh, Julia, I'm sorry." Charlotte didn't know what else to say. Lacie was right. No matter what had happened, Julia had also lost her son.

Julia shook her head. "No. It's my decision. The town didn't need me there as a reminder."

"But she's right," Charlotte said.

"My child is the one who wrecked their lives." Tears welled up in Julia's eyes and trickled down her cheeks. She wiped them away with the edge of the blanket she had wrapped around her.

"Julia . . ." Charlotte didn't bother to argue. "When is Gabe's memorial service? Have you decided on a date yet?"

Once the police had released Gabriel's body, Charlotte stayed with Julia while he was cremated in private. There hadn't been a service yet for him; Julia had wanted to wait for the other families to have theirs first. She didn't want his grave to be there before their children's or loved ones'.

Every decision Julia had made since that fateful day had been with others in mind, always placing their grief, their heartache above her own.

Judging from the amount of food in Julia's kitchen, though, it seemed like she hadn't been forgotten.

Julia shook her head. "I'm not sure I'm going to do one. Who would come? I have no family left, and all my friends . . ." Her voice broke and she couldn't finish.

Charlotte leaned forward and placed her hand on Julia's knee. "Your friends will be there. Maybe not all of them, not yet, but you won't be alone."

"Don't make promises you can't keep."

Charlotte watched as Julia retreated inside of herself even more.

"I will be there, Jules. I promise. I will not leave you alone." That was one promise she vowed to keep: She was not leaving Julia alone. "Do you want me to take care of it? Arrange something private?"

Julia shook her head. "Who would officiate? Not Scott Helman —I couldn't ask that of him."

Charlotte shook her head. No, Scott had done enough. Despite being one of the families who also lost a child on that day, he was also the local pastor and had been at every service held over the past two weeks.

"Not Scott," Charlotte agreed. "Me."

There was a quick flash of hope in Julia's eyes, but it didn't last long.

"I can't. I won't do that to you, Charlotte. You need to be focused on the town, not on me. Just give me some time, okay?"

The defeat in Julia's voice rubbed Charlotte raw, but she knew nothing she said would matter right now.

So she would give her friend time.

2

LACIE HELMAN

Last night I asked Scott to choose between me and the Church. He chose me. I wish he'd chosen the Church.

Lacie read and reread that sentence over and over until her heart sank and she thought she would drown beneath the weight of what she'd done. With her knees tight to her chest, she rested her forehead against the nightgown pulled tight to cover her legs and forced herself not to cry.

Writing it down made it sound so much worse than what it was. She sounded cold, harsh, uncaring, whereas she was anything but.

She loved Scott. They'd been married for over fifteen years and he was one of her best friends.

But she hated the Church and the life they led. Hated the demands placed on Scott, how, no matter how much they planned to have family time, something always came up. Always. It was rare that he could sit down for a meal without getting a phone call or text message asking for his immediate help or advice. It was always a fight to get Scott to agree to shut his phone off during meals and to ignore the ringing of their home phone when people couldn't get him on his cell. The Helmans used to love sitting down as a family and watching the latest cooking show, but now they had to tape everything and wait for when Scott could join them. The Church always came first. Always. Never his family.

Once, she'd loved being a pastor's wife, loved knowing that she was needed and made a difference. She'd grasped hold of Scott's calling and made it her own until she'd forgotten what it was she'd wanted to do with her life, other than being a wife and a mother.

But it wasn't her calling. She couldn't do it anymore. The late nights. The gossip. The single parenting. The pressure to perform and always be *on*.

She wouldn't lie: She'd been surprised at how Scott responded to her ultimatum.

Her or the Church. He chose her.

She should be thrilled. Elated. On cloud nine.

"Mom? Mom? Mom? Mooommmmm . . ."

Lacie sighed, closed her journal, and replaced it in the drawer of her bedside table before her youngest son, Liam, barreled into her room, running as if he were a quarterback, clutching their tabby kitten like a football under his arm.

"Liam, I don't think Butterball likes being held like that."

Her son stopped dead in his tracks and gave her a weird look, as if how could she even question that?

Butterball gave a few weak meows, and Lacie rushed to extract the nearly suffocated cat from Liam's hold and place her down. Liam watched the kitten scamper beneath Lacie's bed, and before he could get down on his hands and knees to go after it, Lacie grabbed her youngest son by the shoulders and steered him back toward her door. She grabbed her housecoat and slipped her feet into the slippers.

"Have you had your breakfast yet?"

"You weren't there." He looked up at her with his big eyes.

"But you're a big boy now, remember? You can pour your own cereal."

His lips pursed and he dug his heels into the carpet. He turned, crossed his arms over his chest, and frowned at her.

"You weren't there," he repeated.

Lacie sighed. "I know I wasn't, but I was coming. Daddy got your cereal down, didn't he?" Scott promised he'd help the kids with breakfast this morning before he went to the church. He also promised he'd call a board meeting for tonight and announce that he was stepping down.

Her stomach twisted in a knot at the thought. She hated herself for making him choose, for making him give up his dream, his passion . . . but she was dying a slow death, and she wasn't sure how much longer she could hang on. Somehow, somewhere, she'd lost herself. Who was Lacie Helman? She had to be more than a mother, more than a pastor's wife . . . but what?

Was the love they shared enough? She used to think so—that as long as they had each other, they could get through anything. But that love . . . it hadn't helped much in the past few years. It hadn't kept her from losing herself, her identity. At what point had she even stopped loving herself?

She donned her housecoat, slipping her arms inside, and then made a tight knot with the belt to hold the edges together. She really needed a new one. Either that or proper pyjamas to walk around the house in. Except this was a school day, which meant even proper pyjamas wouldn't work.

"Listen." She bent down and looked Liam straight in the eyes. "Can you go and pour some cereal into your bowl while Mommy gets dressed? I'll be lickety-split, okay?"

Liam nodded, a deep drop of his head so that his chin almost hit his chest. "Okay," he said.

Lacie smiled at him, leaned forward, and placed a small kiss on his forehead. "That's a good boy."

She headed back into her bedroom, but not before she heard her son call out, "Lickety-split, Mommy."

"Lickety-split, Liam. Promise."

She knew she had maybe two minutes before he rushed back into her room, thinking she'd disappeared somehow.

She threw on yoga pants and a long T-shirt. She'd have a shower later once Emily, Liam's helper, stopped by. She straightened the comforter on the bed and was pulling her hair into a ponytail when Liam's expected panic began.

"Mom? Mommm? Moooommm?" Liam banged on the closed door to her room. When she opened it his hand was in midswing, and instead of connecting with the door, his fist connected with her thigh.

"Oomph," she said. He was quite strong for his age and size. "I'm right here, kiddo. You were supposed to pour your cereal like a big boy, remember?"

"I missed you."

The way he said it, looking up at her with his big blue eyes and his hands cupped beneath his chin, melted her heart.

"Well, you don't have to miss me anymore, 'cause guess what?" Lacie held her hand out to Liam, who grabbed hold.

"What?" His voice bounced off the walls with its vibrancy.

"You don't have to miss me anymore, 'cause I'm right here." She smiled down, knowing exactly how he'd respond.

"Yay!" he shouted. "Wesley . . . hey, Wesley . . . Wessssllllleeeeyyyyy," Liam called out.

Her twelve-year-old son, Wes, poked his head out his bedroom door. "What's up, buddy?"

"Mom's here." Liam smiled, his huge grin stretching from one side of his face to the other.

"Hey, Mom. Sorry, I meant to be downstairs with him, but I slept in."

"It's all good. I figured you'd be tired after last night. You didn't get home until really late with Dad."

Last night was the culmination of everything Lacie had been feeling—the fact that her son had been out until almost midnight because no one else would stay to help Scott clean up after some kid had spray-painted graffiti on the church.

"At least school is almost done, right?" He wore a hopeful look on his face.

"You've a month left, Wes. That's not almost done."

"But it's close."

Ever the optimist, her son. "Yes, it's close. Not close enough that it's okay to be up till midnight on a school night, however."

"Dad needed my help."

Lacie struggled not to roll her eyes. "I'm sure he did. Because there was no one, no adult," she corrected herself, "who could have stayed to help your father."

Liam tugged at her hand, and when she didn't move fast enough, he pulled. "Hungry. Hungry now."

"Sorry," Wes muttered before he closed the door.

Lacie walked away, knowing it wasn't right to take her frustrations out on her son, that he still viewed the Church, the people, as family. His family. God's family. And it was only right to do anything and everything to help those in God's family.

But that wasn't how it was supposed to be. She wasn't sure whether it was disappointment, bitterness, or just plain anger that welled up inside her at the thought.

Since when was it okay for ministers to put the needs of their families last? Since when did the Church have to come first?

She had a niggling worry that Wes would have a hard time understanding why Scott was stepping down from being a pastor. But they would deal with that when the time came. There would be so many questions they'd have to answer, not just from their own children but from others in town. Lacie knew this, but if she were being honest, she wasn't ready for it.

It would have made things so much easier if Scott had chosen the Church. Except, deep down, she knew that wasn't the outcome she wanted. She didn't want to leave her husband, didn't want to destroy their marriage . . . what she wanted was a divorce from the Church.

Kelsie was already downstairs, her head bowed as she devoured mouthfuls of her cereal. She glanced up, but instead of smiling, she spooned more cereal into her already full mouth and then grabbed the box of Lucky Charms on the counter and poured more into her bowl.

"How many bowls is that?" Lacie narrowed her gaze at her thirteen-year-old daughter.

Sheepishly, Kelsie held up three fingers.

Lacie knew she should say something, get upset, lecture her on the values of eating not only a healthy breakfast but a reasonable one, but she couldn't, because Liam dropped to the floor and began his regular dance of flailing and wailing.

She so didn't need this right now. "Please tell me you left some for your brother." She knew from the look on her daughter's face that she hadn't.

"Why, Kelsie? You know that's his favorite. Why couldn't you have left him at least one bowl?"

And just like that, the look on her daughter's face went from mischievous to thunderous.

"It's my favorite too."

Lacie stepped over her son, who continued to throw a temper tantrum on the floor, and reached for the empty cereal box. "I hope there's more in the pantry," she muttered.

Lacie and Scott worked really hard to ensure that they didn't give Liam any special attention compared to their other children, despite his being their only child with Down syndrome. But sometimes it was hard.

"Are you done yet, Liam?" Lacie asked while she searched the pantry for an alternative that would make him stop. Some Special K and Rice Krispies, but no Lucky Charms.

She couldn't wait for this stage to be over. All kids threw

temper tantrums, but Kelsie and Wes seemed to grow out of it pretty early. Not so Liam. He was always a few years behind.

"Hey, man, what's all the commotion about?" Wes ran down the stairs and slid across the floor until he was beside Liam. "I thought maybe we could do something different for breakfast today," he half whispered in a conspiratorial tone.

"Like what?"

"Mom bought some supersecret toaster waffles yesterday and tried to hide them. What do you say we eat them up before she gets a chance to?" Wes turned his head slightly and winked at her. Lacie had to turn away; otherwise Liam would see the smile on her face and know it was all a ruse.

"Secret waffles?" She could hear the excitement in Liam's voice. "Okay."

"Keep it on the down-low, though," Wes whispered.

"Mom, Mom . . . we're going to sneak your waffles." Liam giggled.

Lacie just shook her head and headed into the back, to the freezer, leaving the kids to their breakfast. Once again she was so thankful for Wesley and how patient he was with Liam.

While the kids ate, Lacie got their school bags ready, complete with lunch. It was Wesley's day to bring in a snack for his class, so she'd made some chocolate-chip cookies and placed them in the freezer overnight. Except, as she opened the freezer lid, the bright red Tupperware container she'd used was gone.

"Where're all the cookies I made last night, guys?" she called out.

When no one answered, she sighed before closing the lid and heading back into the kitchen.

"I'm serious. Where are the cookies? Wes has to take them to school today." She looked at Kelsie, who shrugged, and then to Wes and Liam, who shook their heads.

She grabbed her cell phone from the counter and sent Scott a quick text.

Please tell me you didn't take cookies from the freezer this morning.

It didn't take long for him to answer.

I did. Was that okay?

She leaned her head back and stared up at the ceiling. She wasn't even going to ask why—no doubt there was some Bible study or prayer meeting or something and he was just being kind. Everyone probably fawned all over him for being so thoughtful in bringing cookies, and knowing Scott, he'd make sure she got all the glory.

They were for Wesley's class.

I'm sorry! I'll call Anne Marie and ask her to put some cookies aside. Do you want me to drop them off?

And just like that, any frustration she'd felt melted.

Thank you. Tell her I'll grab them.

Yes, he made mistakes, but he was always the first to admit it and try to make it up.

Love you.

She read those words and knew he meant them. He must—he was leaving the Church for her.

See you later. She knew he wanted, needed her to say it back to him. And really, saying those three words he needed to hear this morning shouldn't be so difficult. Of course she loved him. She always would. But she didn't feel it right now. She'd just asked him to make a major decision regarding their marriage and he had . . . but did he think that erased all her feelings, her anger and her frustration?

She sighed. Of course he did, because that was how he thought. She'd asked him to make a choice and he'd made it without any hesitation. Because he loved her.

Love you too, she texted back.

"Okay, guys, we need to get ready soon. As soon as you finish your breakfast, we'll make a pit stop at Sweet Bakes and grab some cookies from Anne Marie."

"Did Dad take the ones you made last night?" Wesley asked.

"I'm afraid so, kiddo."

"Can we get some for home, too?" Kelsie asked.

"Oh, I think we might be able to do that." She should also pick up one of Anne Marie's chocolate croissants as well. And maybe even a pie for Scott for when he came home after his meeting.

They were about to head out the door when Kelsie stopped her.

"Um, you're not going out like that, are you?"

Lacie glanced down at her yoga pants and T-shirt and chuckled. "What? You don't like my Mickey Mouse shirt?"

Kelsie's brows rose. "You look fat."

Inside, Lacie wanted to scream and tell her daughter to mind her own business and accept her the way she was, but she didn't. She didn't stand up for herself, didn't put her daughter in her place . . . didn't do any of the things she should have done. Instead, she plastered a smile on her face like a good Christian should do and stepped backward. It didn't matter that Kelsie had been on this kick lately about appearances and was starting that stage where it didn't take much for Lacie to embarrass her. It didn't matter that what her daughter had said might be true.

"Give me two minutes and I'll get changed." She gave in. Again. One day she wouldn't.

She threw on jeans, a top, and a light sweater and ran back downstairs. Just as she was locking the door, her cell phone rang.

"Hey, there." If it had been anyone else she wouldn't have answered, but Charlotte Stone was one of her *girls*, among her best friends.

"I'm sure you're rushing out the door, but do you have time to chat later?" Charlotte asked.

With the phone tucked tight against her shoulder, Lacie headed to the vehicle. Wes was helping Liam into his car seat while Kelsie was brushing her hair.

"Depends on when. Emily will be here in an hour, but I think Scott's coming home early today." She loved when Emily came to the house to work with Liam. Their support home worker was a godsend, and Lacie still couldn't believe they'd received state funding for her help as easily as they had.

"Is he sick?" Lacie heard the concern in Charlotte's voice.

"No," she hedged, unsure of what or how much to say.

"Everything okay?"

"Everything is good." She used her pastor's-wife voice, the one that pretended everything was fine, she was happy, and life couldn't be better.

"Don't you use that tone with me, Lacie Helman."

She smiled. Trust Charlotte to know when she wasn't telling the truth. "I have to run and get cookies from Sweet Bakes. It's Wes's day to bring snacks, but," she tried to not sound bitter, "Scott took the cookies I made into the office with him."

"That was nice of Scott—I'm sure everyone in the church office appreciated it."

Lacie sighed and changed the subject. "I'm really looking forward to our girls' night. I need it more than you can know."

"I'm looking forward to it as well. A night away, with no expectations and just plain girlfriend fun . . . it couldn't come sooner. Give me a shout later, okay? Or come by Gina's after Emily arrives. I'm meeting Jenn for coffee."

Lacie told her she'd think about it and then twisted to make sure Liam was buckled in properly.

"What kind of cookies should we get?" she asked while Charlotte's words rang in her mind. *That was nice of him.* Of course it was. Except he'd walked in last night after the men's Bible study and seen her packing them up. He'd even managed to sneak a few out of the container before she put it in the freezer. He knew they weren't meant for him or the church or anyone else other than Wesley's class.

She knew he'd just forgotten; he basically admitted that in his text earlier. But it still upset her. One more example of Scott placing something ahead of his own family. Why couldn't someone else provide the cookies? Why couldn't someone else bake something and tell Scott to take it home for once, rather than the other way around?

No one in Stillwater Bay would have agreed with her, much less understood her frustration. They all hailed Scott as one of the best pastors to ever come to Stillwater Faith Community Church. They praised him on a continual basis for how he put the church first, how dedicated he was to not only the town, but the church, the members, the families.

And now she was asking him to be dedicated to his own and only his own. Everyone in town would hate her, but would they understand? Would her friends, at least? She had a feeling they would, that when they found out tomorrow night what she'd done, they would be on her side one hundred percent.

While the kids called out every type of cookie they knew Anne Marie made, Lacie drove across First Bridge Street, breathing in the crisp morning air. She loved where they lived—on Whidbey Island off the coast of Washington, close to the water, where the breeze carried the smell of the ocean in from beyond the bay. But she longed for the days when they used to live closer to the water, where she could hear and see the waves crashing along the shore. The parsonage where they'd first lived when they moved here was nestled among the cottages on the shores of South Beach; she and Scott used to sit out on the back porch and watch the sun set over the waves and dream about what their lives would be.

"Are we decided then on our cookies?" She turned in her seat after parking across from Sweet Bakes and winked at her kids.

"I am!" Liam yelled out. He pulled at his buckles, straining to get out, and then laughed as Wes tickled him.

"Watch for cars." Lacie climbed out and held the door open for the kids. She was glad the street was quiet, because she knew the moment Liam was out of his seat, he would try to run.

"Liam," she called out to grab his attention. "Should we pick out a cookie for Miss Emily?"

His eyes widened as she held out her hand for him to take. Liam loved his helper; he thought she was not only beautiful but smart and kind, and he was always coloring pictures for when she came over three times a week to work with him. Next year they were going to sign him up for kindergarten at Stillwater Elementary, where Emily would go in and work with him in a class setting.

Wesley held the door open so they could all file in, and the minute Liam entered the bakery, he ran right toward the back, around the corner, and tackled Anne Marie, who luckily was waiting for him.

"Hey, big guy." She leaned down and wrapped her arms around him. "How come you don't come visit me anymore?"

Liam gazed up, his eyes wide. "Mommy says you don't want me ruining your pies again." His lips pushed out into a pout but quickly turned into a smile when Anne Marie laughed and nuzzled the top of his head.

The last time Lacie had brought Liam into the bakery, he'd tackled Anne Marie while her hands were full of homemade pies. Liam grabbed her so hard that the pies fell out of her hands and landed on the floor.

"You can't ruin a pie; it's not possible. In fact, how about I show you what I did to a pie this morning." She reached for Liam's hand and pulled him to the side. Lacie made her way to the counter and leaned over it so she could see as well.

On a pie plate sat what looked like a cherry explosion. There was a little bit of crust, but basically cherries covered everything else. Anne Marie handed Liam a plastic fork, and then grabbed one for herself and stuck it in the pie.

"Try it and let me know if it tastes okay?" She smiled down at Liam before glancing over to Lacie and winking. "You too, Kelsie and Wes. I originally meant this pie for your dad, but now . . . well, who said we can't have pie for breakfast?" She handed the other two forks before she wiped her hands on her apron and approached Lacie.

"That man of yours sure did it this morning, huh?"

"Don't even get me started." Lacie smiled, thankful to Anne Marie for not starting off praising her husband. Most people never saw the man, only the title. Put *Reverend* in front of a name and then a man could do no wrong.

"I put a box together and added a mixture of cookies. I'm trying out a new recipe with caramel, and made sure they're all peanut-free."

"Thanks. I told the kids they could pick out some cookies and I'll take them home too. And maybe a pie for dessert."

"Sure thing. I'll have your order for the fair committee ready for tonight as well. Want me to drop it off on my way home?"

"If you don't mind, that would be great."

Each year, Stillwater Bay held a summer fair that began on the last day of school and ran for three days. Lacie was part of the committee, and she loved their meetings. It meant a rare night out that had nothing to do with the church.

Anne Marie gave her a smile, and then turned. "Okay, kiddos, I hear we have some cookies to pick for when you're at home. Who wants to go first?"

Lacie stood to the side and watched her children as they made their choices. Anne Marie was amazing with kids. She helped out with the Sunday school program at church and was always the first to volunteer for any child events in the town. She once told Lacie that she considered the children of Stillwater her family, since she didn't have any of her own.

"Add it to your tab?" Anne Marie called out as she boxed everything up and placed them in bags. Lacie nodded. Scott came in weekly to pay their tab—things the church ordered as well as their own family's items.

"Are we still on for our girls' night tomorrow?" Anne Marie asked.

"At this point only God himself could cancel it. I think it's at Grey Rose." Lacie didn't really care where they met—as long as there were no husbands or kids around.

"Right, I almost forgot. Go figure Jenn would pick there. Seems to be her favorite spot for us."

Every month Jennifer Crowne, Julia Berry, Charlotte, Anne Marie, and Lacie got together. They talked, they argued, and they reminded themselves that they were more than just mothers, wives, the mayor, or business owners. It was a night Lacie always looked forward to. Twice a year they planned a weekend trip, and tonight they were going to plan their summer one. They always did it in August, before school started and after things started to quiet down from all the summer activities in town.

"Have a good day, kids." Anne Marie handed her the bags and Lacie herded her children out of the store. She shook her head when she noticed a cookie in each of the kids' hands, and when she looked back, Anne Marie had the widest smile on her face.

Today was going to be the mother of all sugar overloads, and it was Friday, which meant the kids came home early. Lacie would need to figure out a healthy lunch for Liam or he was going to crash later on from all the sugar, and a crashed Liam was never a good thing.

The ride to school was relatively quiet, thanks to the cookies the kids were eating. Lacie drove past the church and saw Scott standing in his office window, as if he were waiting for them to drive by. She honked the horn; the kids all waved and Scott waved back.

There was still enough time that if she drove home, they could walk to school and make it before the bell rang.

"Want to walk or have me drop you off?"

"Drop off, please," Kelsie and Wes called out at the same time.

Lacie drove past Bay Street, where they lived right on the corner, and made her way to Pelican Street. There was quite the lineup of cars waiting to turn left toward the school.

"Or I could drop you off here?"

"Sure, that works," Wesley said.

She pulled over to the curb and waited for the kids to unbuckle themselves and gather their belongings. She handed Wes the bag with his cookies.

"Have a great day, okay? Be safe, play smart, and remember I love you." She said the same thing to them every morning. It was her little prayer over them, and the few times she'd forgotten to say it, Kelsie had gotten upset and asked her whether she still loved them.

"Love you, Mom!" Kelsie called out.

"See you after school, Mom," Wesley said.

"Bye, Wes. By, Kels. Bye, bye, bye," Liam called out as they shut the door.

Lacie watched them walk down the sidewalk and waited until they had crossed the street before she pulled out and drove home.

A heaviness lodged in her stomach and she tried to ignore it. Today was going to be a good day. She was going to go home, wait for Emily to arrive, and then have a shower and maybe lock herself away in her room for a bit before Scott came home. She needed time to think, to really register the change that was about to take place.

If she were really the kind of wife Scott needed, the kind of pastor's wife their church needed, she would be with Scott right now at the church, standing by him, going to various meetings and lending her support. But she wasn't. She tried—she really did—but the harder she tried, the more she lost herself.

It was selfish of her, but she was glad she wasn't going to be there. Today wouldn't be easy for him. He was long overdue for a sabbatical, and they'd both agreed last night that he would take that first—so that there would be a source of income for them while they figured the next step out. But was he having any doubts? Did he wish that he'd responded to her in a different way?

How would things be between them now? What kind of wife

was she to force her husband to make a choice?

She remembered a conference she'd gone to a few years ago for pastors and their wives. She'd sat among some of the biggest names in their ministry and listened to the wives as they talked about standing beside their men, being their support. Lacie took to heart that God had created her not to follow after her husband but to stand by his side . . . to be his strength when he was weak, to urge him on when he needed help, to hold him when he couldn't be strong. But she'd walked away from there feeling as if she were missing something.

Everything had been focused on how she could support her husband. But what about him supporting her? Why was it only a one-way street? Why did she need to make the sacrifices when he couldn't? Why was it okay for her to expect him to put the Church first? She knew she was part of the problem. She'd let this go on for years, never demanding anything different from him, not wanting to be another burden. She quit her job as an administrative assistant when Kelsie was born and never looked back. Not until recently, when she realized she had no life other than the roles of mother and pastor's wife.

She felt sick inside. Sick because of how she felt. Sick because she knew that after today, their lives would never be the same and it was all her fault.

"Going to be a good day, right, Mommy?" Liam asked her as she parked the car in the driveway.

"It's going to be a good day, Liam. The best."

As she helped him out of his car seat, he jumped forward and wrapped his arms around her neck.

"You're the bestest mommy ever," he said to her, his nose touching hers.

"I'm trying, honey. I'm trying." She gave him a kiss, and then untangled his hands from her neck before leading him up to their front door.

She was trying.

3

Charlotte Stone

The Past: Friday, May 31

Black or blue? Charlotte held up the dresses, one in each hand, and couldn't decide what to wear.

"Blue." Jordan, her husband, walked into the closet and reached for a tie from the rack. "Think this will be okay?" He held in his hand a pink-and-black checked tie.

"I thought you were going to go with a more relaxed feel on Fridays?" She hung the blue dress back up. It was a wraparound and didn't hide anything, whereas the black one had a higher waist, which meant she could eat a couple of scones at Gina's and not have it show.

"I've got a few parent-teacher interviews this afternoon." Jordan was the principal at Stillwater Public School. They made a good team, running the town together, if Charlotte did say so herself. While she worried about keeping the town strong and getting them through the long winter months until Stillwater's summer tourist season began, her husband focused on the families, especially the kids. Between the two of them, they were able to handle most of the situations that arose around town.

Charlotte handed Jordan her black dress so that she could help him with his tie. She loved a tie on a man, and had given him this one a few months ago, after he found out he was nominated for an award through the local school district. She loved that he always looked good.

"I knew you would pick the black dress."

She tightened the knot around his neck, smoothed the fabric, and smiled. "So why suggest the blue one?"

"To see if you'd actually wear something I liked." He leaned forward and placed a kiss on her cheek.

She caught his little dig but decided to ignore it.

"I don't need you to dress me," she reminded him.

"I know you don't. You don't need much from me; it's why I love you so much." He smiled at her before he walked out of their closet and into their bedroom. She followed after him, a bit bothered by his comment.

"What do you mean, I don't need much from you? You make me sound . . ."

"Independent? You haven't changed in the ten years we've been married. Is that such a bad thing? You're very self-sufficient, able to handle things on your own, and you don't need me to tell you what to do or how to do it," he continued while he opened a box on his dresser and chose a pair of cuff links. "I can't tell you how many calls Tyler gets from his wife on a daily basis, asking his opinion on this or that. Especially asking what he wants for dinner."

Tyler Redding was the vice principal at Stillwater Public School, and Jordan's best friend.

Charlotte really didn't see the issue; nor did she feel like hearing any gossip about Tyler and his marriage. "On that note, what would you like for dinner tonight?" She gave Jordan a wink before she slipped back into the closet and began getting dressed. With the warmer weather, leggings weren't needed, thank God.

"I thought we were meeting at Fred's after work?"

"We are. I was only teasing."

"Or we could drive up the coast, stop in at our favorite bed-and-breakfast, and enjoy a weekend away from everything?" Jordan stood behind her and helped her with the zipper.

"I'm busy tomorrow night. Remember? It's my monthly girls' night out." She couldn't wait. They always had so much fun. It was Jenn's turn to pick and she'd chosen the Grey Rose. Next month it was Charlotte's turn, and she already had the perfect place picked out: She'd heard about a new chocolate bar that had opened up in Seattle and was hoping to convince the girls to try it out.

"What about Sunday then? Just go for a drive?"

"Sure. Want me to order a picnic lunch?"

"From Gina's?" Jordan's eyes lit up. "See if she'll make her famous couscous salad again." Jordan checked himself in the mirror and then grabbed his wallet, stuffing it in the back pocket of his pants. "I need to run, but I'll meet you tonight. Oh, I made coffee."

Once he left, Charlotte finished getting dressed, chose a pair of dress sandals to wear, and headed downstairs, where half a pot of coffee waited. She poured herself a cup and then headed into her study.

On Fridays she liked to take it a bit easy. She worked from home for the first few hours and then headed into her office downtown. Today she had a few proposals to read over, and then she'd meet Jenn over at Gina's for coffee.

The first thing she wanted to do was see what kind of help she could get Tyler's wife, Sandy. With a new baby and a toddler, the poor woman was probably exhausted, and it wasn't so much that she was needy, but just that she needed help—help her husband no doubt never thought to give her. Charlotte had never really liked Tyler—there was something about him that always set her on edge. She couldn't put her finger on it . . . it might be the way he talked down to women, or how he expected Sandy to wait on him hand and foot, but the fact that he was one of her husband's best friends didn't help.

Jordan and Tyler knew each other from college. There was a history she couldn't break between them. So many times during the early years of their marriage, Tyler would show up on one of their nights out, or pop over late at night and stay for hours on end, drinking and being loud while she was trying to sleep.

"Jordan's glad I'm not needy," she mumbled to herself. That bothered her, and she wasn't exactly sure why. Of course she wasn't needy; she never wanted to be one of *those* wives. But it was the way he'd said it. . . . What if something happened in their lives and she needed him? Would he find her bothersome? Irritating? Her independence and self-reliance were things he'd found attractive when they'd first met.

She glanced at the time and picked up the phone.

"Hey, girl," she said once Jenn answered.

"I was waiting for you to call."

Charlotte leaned back in her chair. "Really? Why is that?"

"Oh, I don't know. It's Friday and you're antsy without being in the office. What time are we meeting at Gina's?" There was a teasing tilt to Jenn's voice. Her best friend knew her way too well.

"How about after you drop the kids off at school?"

Charlotte waited for a few seconds while she heard banging on the other end of the phone.

"What's going on?"

Jenn grunted and swore beneath her breath, and then Charlotte heard the phone drop. There was more muttering, a bit more swearing, and then the sound of running water drowned out anything else Jenn had to say.

Charlotte waited, scenarios running through her head as to what had just happened. No doubt she burned her fingers or hand while taking cookies, some pastry, or muffins out of the oven. It was very rare that Jenn didn't bake something first thing in the morning.

"I forgot to use an oven mitt. Augh. Gina's, after school, right?"

"If that works." That gave her time to get a little bit of work done, but not enough time to get swamped.

"Totally works. There's something I want to talk to you about too, so it's great timing."

Charlotte perked up at this. "Oh, really? Like what?"

"Just . . ." Jenn's voice lowered. "Remember that thing I told you I was going to do?"

Charlotte sat straight up in her chair. "You did it? I thought you were only thinking about it. Are you sure?"

The sound of a long puff of air came through the phone.

"No, I'm not sure. But I have to do something."

Charlotte leaned back in her chair. "What's your end goal in all this? A wake-up call, or are you actually going to leave him?"

Charlotte knew Jenn was unhappy in her marriage, but she honestly never thought she'd follow through with doing anything about it. Jenn and Robert were a team, similar to her and Jordan. They were the foundation of this town—Robert worked on the town council and Jenn took care of the volunteer committee for the summer fair—and to be honest, Charlotte wasn't sure how to react right now: as a friend or as the mayor, who knew there would be huge consequences. Robert and Jenn were a team, and Charlotte needed them to remain that way, as callous as that sounded.

"I . . ." Jenn paused. "The kids are up. Let's chat later."

"Are you okay?" There was something in Jenn's voice . . . something Charlotte hadn't heard in a long time.

"Just . . . later."

Charlotte heard Jenn's kids in the background. Little Bobby's voice was high-pitched, and from the loud thump she heard, she could picture him jumping off the stairs. Charity's voice was a bit muffled, but Charlotte knew Jenn's focus was now on her children. The way it should be.

Charlotte hung up the phone and quashed a little tingle of jealousy as she thought of Jenn's dedication to her family. Together, she and Jordan had made a decision years ago not to have children, a choice she'd never regretted. Her focus was on her town, on the families of Stillwater Bay. She knew that throwing their own children into the mix would only complicate matters. And when she made a decision, she embraced it with every fiber in her being. It was what made her so good at her job.

Once, years ago, her mother had told her she never wanted grandchildren. At the time, Charlotte had been a bit annoyed, and accused her mom of taking her personal hesitations toward Jordan too far, but then she'd said something that shook Charlotte to the core.

Don't do to your children what we did to you. It's not worth it. Love them enough to not put them through it.

Charlotte grew up believing the feeling of love could never be trusted, that it never lasted and her mom was right. When she thought about Jordan . . . They worked well as a team, but that *thing,* that *feeling* that was supposed to be between a husband and wife . . . it wasn't there anymore, and she felt a little empty inside because of it.

Charlotte's cell phone vibrated with a text message.

Good time to call?

She shook her head at the timing of her mom's message before picking up her cordless phone and calling her directly.

"I hope I'm not bothering you," her mother said in her usual quiet voice.

"Not at all. I was actually going to call you later," Charlotte fibbed.

"I'm sure I was on your list of things to do today." The sigh from her mother had Charlotte clenching her teeth.

"You're never on my 'list,' Mother." It was the same

conversation they had every week. Her mother would sigh and claim she didn't want to bother Charlotte, whom she knew had to be busy, and Charlotte would reassure her that she was never a bother.

Every single time.

"I was wondering if you'd both like to come by tonight for dinner?"

Charlotte's brows rose.

"I was just there on Monday." She made it a point to stop by the retirement home as often as she could.

"Oh, I know. But. . ." Her voice trailed off.

"But what?" This wasn't like her mother. She rarely asked after Jordan, and when she did, it was only to be polite when others were around.

"Well, you see, some of the ladies here . . ."

The silence stretched on between them until Charlotte couldn't handle it any longer.

"The ladies what?"

Her mother sighed. "The ladies would like him to come by with some of the kids again."

"Then have Dorothea Peters call the school. She did last time." Dorothea was the manager of the Stillwater Retirement Home and had often requested that Jordan bring students over to interact with the seniors there. The kids would sing songs, put on plays, and spend time with their family members.

"Well, see, that's the problem. She has, but Jordan hasn't returned her calls."

"And you're willing to spend an evening with him over dinner in order to convince him?" Charlotte doubted that very much.

"Well . . . could you maybe talk to him?" The hope in her mother's voice was almost too much.

For some reason, her mom didn't like Charlotte's husband. She said it was her motherly intuition, that she knew the moment she'd first met Jordan and he'd forgotten to wipe his shoes on the doormat, but sometimes Charlotte wondered. Her mother took to most people, welcoming them with open arms . . . except the man Charlotte chose to be her husband. It didn't help that when Jordan first asked her to marry him, he'd forgotten to honor the time-old tradition of asking her father, despite the fact that they were both old enough to make their own decisions and her mother and father had been divorced for more than ten years and barely spoke to each other. It didn't matter—her mother was still deeply offended. And then, while she and Jordan were planning their wedding, her mother had wanted to be involved. Not realizing that there was a special way to handle her mother, Jordan had been up-front and reminded her that this wasn't her wedding to plan; it was Charlotte's. Throughout the years, things had not improved, and Charlotte had just learned to leave it alone.

"Yes, I'll talk to him."

"Good. Why don't you come over for dinner then?"

But not Jordan. Go figure.

"I already have dinner plans. But I can pop over later today if you're free." Charlotte opened her calendar and looked to see when she had time in the afternoon.

"Oh, that won't work. There's a Scrabble tournament today."

Scrabble.

"Okay, well, how about I take you out for breakfast tomorrow?"

"As long as you have time, dear. I don't want to get in the way. You're always so busy."

And here we go again.

"Never too busy for you."

"Well, only if you're sure. Maybe ask Julia to come too? It's been awhile since I've seen her."

"Julia? Aren't you still doing your weekly coffee with her?" Charlotte had first met Julia when the other woman had worked at the retirement home as the resident manager.

"Well . . . we kind of put it on hold, with all the issues she's been having with her boy and all." Her mother hedged a bit on that sentence, and Charlotte picked up on it right away.

"What do you mean, issues?" And why hadn't Julia told her about this?

"Oh, you know . . . he's been getting blamed for all that disgusting artwork some kid is doing all over town. But it's not him; it can't be. He has issues, but he's not a bad kid."

The graffiti was being blamed on Gabriel? Why didn't Charlotte know about this? The last she'd heard, it was a small group of boys from another town on a joyride that had already ended weeks ago.

"Are you sure?"

"Well, of course I am. I may be old, but I'm not senile, you know."

There were two sides to the coin she called Mother: Either she played the role of being meek and mild and downright pathetic, or she took offense to any little thing. What had happened to the strong, utterly independent, opinionated woman who had raised her? The doctor said it was just old age and normal, but Charlotte wasn't so sure.

"I'll give her a call and see if she can join us, okay?"

"Well, don't go out of your way."

Charlotte shook her head. "I'll see you tomorrow, Mom."

Pushing thoughts of her mother to the background, Charlotte turned on her computer and pulled up her e-mails. Systematically she went through them, labeling them in terms of importance and then placing them into folders to be dealt with later. She moved a number of them into Sheila's folder and marked them as unread, knowing her assistant would handle them later on. She made sure to e-mail Jordan about her mother's request, and then her thoughts turned to the dinner tomorrow night. It'd been a few days since she'd last chatted with Lacie, and Charlotte wondered how she was doing. She'd seen some notes from her assistant about Lacie volunteering to take on some family events this summer for the town, but Charlotte was worried that she was taking on way too much.

As the pastor's wife from Stillwater Faith Community Church, the largest church in Stillwater after the Catholic Church, Lacie was the person everyone went to when it came to women or mother issues in the community. Lacie not only helped to run a mothers'-day-out group during the week, but held parenting classes through the church as well.

She picked up the phone to call the other woman and caught her just as she was heading out the door. When she asked whether Lacie had time to chat later, Charlotte found out Scott planned to come home early.

"Is he sick?" she asked. Scott rarely left the church early. A few times, Lacie had grumbled about the fact that he seemed more married to the Church than to her.

"No," Lacie hedged.

"Everything okay?" Charlotte didn't want to prod too much, but she had a feeling she needed to.

"Everything is good."

"Don't you use that tone with me, Lacie Helman." She hated when Lacie used her pastor's-wife voice she'd perfected over the years. They chatted a bit longer before Charlotte asked, "Why don't you come by Gina's after Emily arrives? I'm meeting Jenn for coffee."

Once they hung up, Charlotte glanced down at an updated proposal on changes to their summer festival. She couldn't wait for the festival to begin. This year would be their greatest one yet, and despite saying that every year, she really believed it. Jordan had some excellent ideas on how to better incorporate the school grounds this year, which worked great with their need to expand. The annual parade always started from the school parking lot and ended at the community center parking lot.

There were so many activities planned this summer to help draw in vacationing families, and Charlotte was excited. The more families who came to Stillwater Bay for their holidays meant a better fiscal year for the businesses.

And when everyone succeeded, she knew she'd done her job.

Which reminded her, she needed to talk to Julia Berry, the owner of the Treasure Chest and one of her close friends. Julia was a godsend to her in more ways than Charlotte would ever admit. They'd gone through a few rough patches in their friendship, especially after they'd first met.

Charlotte had literally bumped into the woman at the retirement home as Julia came out of her mom's room, giggling like a schoolgirl. Her mom had taken to Julia, at that time the new resident manager, and that piqued Charlotte's interest, since her mother didn't take to many people anymore. Every time she went to visit her, her mother always had Julia at her side, whether it was in her room or sharing a pot of tea in the cafeteria. Eventually Charlotte asked the woman out to Gina's for coffee one day, and they just hit it off.

Their friendship grew over the next month or two, until suddenly Julia stopped taking her calls and made it very obvious she didn't want anything to do with Charlotte.

Charlotte didn't let it bother her much. Things were tense at home, and Jordan had started to talk about looking for another job and moving, an idea Charlotte was dead-set against. Stillwater Bay was their home. Her home. She wasn't moving.

It wasn't until a year or so later, when Julia came to the town hall to lease store space for her new shop, that they picked up their friendship again. They never really spoke of what had happened in the past, and anytime Charlotte mentioned Gabriel in passing, Julia would steer the subject away, until Charlotte realized their friendship would be social and not intimate. Which was okay with her. She had enough close friends, like Lacie and Jenn, who knew enough about her personal life; she didn't need to pour her heart out to someone else.

Charlotte wanted to talk to Julia about a business idea: She'd spoken with Ethan Poole, the manager of the clubhouse up at the golf course, and he'd agreed to host a few of the more upscale items from Julia's boutique that would appeal to women golfers. Charlotte was excited about the opportunity and knew Julia would be as well.

With that added to her list of things to do, Charlotte pushed her chair back and smiled.

Nothing made her happier than when she had reasons to focus on the town. Nothing.

HAVEN'T READ STILLWATER SHORES? ORDER YOUR COPY TODAY.

Turn the page for an excerpt from STILLWATER RISING —>

STILLWATER

A Novel

RISING

STEENA HOLMES

NEW YORK TIMES BESTSELLING AUTHOR

STILLWATER RISING

STILLWATER BAY SERIES

STEENA HOLMES

Published by Lake Union Publishing, Seattle www.apub.com

ISBN-13: 9781477825150

ISBN-10: 1477825150

Cover design by Kimberly Glyder Design

Library of Congress Control Number: 2014937381 Printed in the United States of America

ISBN: 978-0-9920555-5-4

A NOTE FROM STEENA

If ever there was a book that I wish more readers could read…it would be Stillwater Rising.
There's something about this story that hits hearts in such a real way - sadly, the subject of this book is something we hear about too often in the news.
My goal with Stillwater Rising was NOT to focus on the event that led up to this story - the school shooting - but rather focus on the aftermath - primarily, the healing that needs to come from such a tragic event.

While I am unable to provide the full story within this boxed set - I did receive permission from my publisher to include the first five chapters of Stillwater Rising in this collection! I hope you will enjoy these chapters and don't worry - there's a buy link so you can continue on with the story!

Stillwater Rising

This book is dedicated to the families who have been affected, in one way or another, by an event similar to what has happened to this fictional town. Your loss can never be adequately shared, but I am humbled by your strength.

1

JENNIFER CROWNE

THE WATER in the bay rippled with the push of a breeze that wafted in through the open kitchen window. With her eyes closed, Jenn welcomed the morning kiss on her cheeks as the air surrounded her. She tightened a shaggy brown housecoat around her body and waited for the flow of the coffeepot to slow enough for her to fill her mug. The drip of each drop into the pot of liquid rang in her ears, along with the steady tick of their old grandfather clock down the hall. Every small sound intensified against the morbid stillness in the house, a facade that ate her insides every second there was no noise, no laughter.

She leaned down, planted her elbows on the wood block of her island, and stared out their large bay windows that overlooked Stillwater Bay. Her husband had built their house on the cliff with the bay on one side and the town of Stillwater on the other. Glass windows filled three-quarters of their home. Rob claimed it was so they could see everything around them, but to Jenn, there was no place to hide.

Once she had loved the openness. Now she hated it.

A light fog hugged the waters below as it drifted out with the current. Every day since *that day* a fog had covered the shore. As if the bay itself was in mourning, a thought that comforted Jenn more than she wanted to admit.

A light scuffle and creak from upstairs alerted her that Charity, her thirteen-year-old daughter, was awake. A glance at the clock confirmed it was still early, barely past six in the morning. Jenn sighed at the thought of another long day when she had to be stronger than she was.

She'd been dreading this day since the letter came in the mail.

She checked the chocolate-chip muffins she'd pulled out of the oven earlier to make sure they were cool enough, just as her daughter came down the stairs.

"Good morning." Jenn straightened and held out her arms. Despite the dark circles beneath Charity's eyes, her gaze was bright, almost to the point of feverish.

"Morning," Charity mumbled as Jenn gave her a hug. She pressed her lips against Charity's forehead to test for a fever.

"Can we go in a bit early today?" Charity pulled away and reached for a muffin from the tray.

"I was actually thinking . . . why don't we go into the city for the day? We could go see a movie, do some shopping . . ." Heading into the city was one of the last things she wanted to do, but it was better than the alternative.

"You can't be serious?"

It had been a gradual change, but the sweet, innocent daughter Jenn once knew was gone. She saw glimpses, when Charity didn't think anyone was looking, but gone was the charming little girl Jenn knew, and in her place was a hormonal, surly teenager who didn't seem to remember what it meant to respect her parents.

"Yes, Charity. I'm serious. It could be"—she struggled to find the appropriate wording—"fun?"

"Shopping? Fun? No thanks. I'd rather go to school, Mom." The exasperation was quite clear in Charity's voice.

Jenn's shoulders sagged. The school.

"It's going to be a madhouse, so I'd like to get there a bit early if we could. Mandy and I planned to meet up so we could go in together."

Jenn didn't know how her daughter did it. How she could be ready to head back into *that place* so soon.

Just the thought of the school, the mere mention of its name, brought vivid images to mind, images Jenn knew would haunt her for the rest of her life. Thank God Charity would be going to high school in Midland in the fall.

"Amanda's going? Of course she is." There was no reason she wouldn't. "Well . . . I thought your dad would take you. Didn't he say that? He knows I can't . . . ," Jenn sighed at the dubious look on her daughter's face. Of course he wasn't going to take her.

"Mom, you have to drive me. You can do it."

"I'm sorry. I don't think I can," Jenn managed to whisper before she took a deep breath and fortified herself.

What was it Robert had said to her last night? That people looked up to her, counted on her to be strong. But who would be strong for her? Not her husband. He wanted to pretend it had never happened, burying himself in his work instead of allowing himself to grieve for what they had lost.

Her gaze drifted to the abundance of floral arrangements and cards that littered her house. She wanted to throw them all out, rip up the cards she couldn't bear to read with the well-meaning words written on them, and burn them until she choked on the smoke.

The grief counselor had told her that one day she'd want to read those cards, that the words written would give her the strength to remember, to get past the nightmare she lived. Soon she'd have to throw out the dead arrangements, the ones that had withered, but even those she couldn't touch. Every time the local deliveryman rang her doorbell, she had him place the vases on the foyer table for either Robert or Charity.

"How's the muffin?" Jenn changed the subject as she took another piece of her muffin and nibbled on it.

"Edible," Charity mumbled as she reached for her second one. Jenn shook her head but kept quiet. *Pick your battles,* her counselor had said.

"Are you ready?"

Charity shook her head as she glanced down at the pyjamas she wore.

"No, I mean, are you sure you're ready to go to the school today? I'm sure Amanda or even Principal Stone could gather your things for you."

"Mandy's mom says we can either be the victor or the victim. And if we don't face our fears, then they'll soon control us."

Of course Amanda's mother said that. It wasn't her child who had been gunned down at the public school. It wasn't Amanda's mother who had found her son facedown in his own blood.

"And is that what you're doing? Facing your fears?"

"I'm not afraid of anything." Charity's head popped up, and her chin jutted out.

Jenn sagged against the counter and turned her attention back to the scene outside her windows. The water in the bay beckoned her, soothed her.

"I wish I could say the same thing," she whispered. She was afraid of everything lately, it seemed. Before the shooting, she knew what she wanted in life. In fact, she'd taken steps to change her life, to be more in charge. She thought about the envelope sitting in her desk drawer and wondered if she'd ever get back to the woman she used to be.

"So can we? Mom? Hello-o?"

Jenn shook her head and refocused. "I'm sorry?"

Throwing her hands up in frustration, Charity just frowned and stood there with her hands on her hips.

“Right. School. No. I don’t think you should go.” Jenn filled her mug with coffee, grabbed another muffin, and started to head over to the breakfast nook when her daughter’s voice stopped her.

“But Dad said . . .”

Jenn turned. “I don’t care what your father said. I’m not taking you. If he wanted you to go, then he should have been here to drive you.”

She’d had this argument with Robert last night. She’d suggested instead of going into the office in the wee hours like he normally did to get a head start on work, he should stay home and they would have breakfast as a family, then they could deal with this if it came up. Apparently he hadn’t believed her when she said she wasn’t going to drive Charity to the school.

“That’s not fair.”

“You should know by now, life isn’t fair.”

“I’m calling Dad.” Charity reached for the phone. “Yes, great idea.”

A letter had been mailed last week to all the families letting them know about the school opening the last Friday before summer vacation officially began. A day for closure and remembrance. The day was going to include games and outdoor activities, but opening the school—for even a short period of time—had nothing to do with supporting their children and everything to do with maintaining the pretense that their town was learning to move forward.

“But Dad—” Charity half turned away from her as she spoke to Robert on the phone.

Jenn watched as her daughter’s face crumpled. She breathed a small sigh of relief as her daughter hung up the phone. Jenn didn’t say anything, but she was thankful Robert backed her up on this even if he didn’t agree with her.

“He can’t drive me. He has a bunch of meetings today. Which totally sucks.” Charity pushed items around on the island.

"There's no reason to go, Charity, you know that. If it's just to see your friends, then you can do that anytime."

"That's not it."

"Then what is it? Explain it to me. Why are you so insistent to return to that school?"

"You don't understand." Charity lowered her gaze. "Please, Mom, will you just take me?"

Jenn shook her head. "Please don't ask me again."

She never wanted to step foot back in that school. Ever. She doubted there would ever be a day when she didn't drive by without remembering, without the sinking weight of depression and grief hitting her.

Robert had asked her how long she was going to be like this. When she asked him what he meant, he only stared at her. Then he said the words she wasn't ready to hear.

"You've lost yourself. Little by little, and I don't even think you care."

But she did care. She did. But it had only been a month since she'd lost her son. A month. Of course she wasn't going to be her usual self.

A week ago today, the town had held a funeral service for the students who had been murdered in a fit of rage by a local teen. Weeks before, each family had held their own private services. A time to mourn the loss of their children in a senseless act. There were so many questions without answers, so much anger, hurt, and fear.

Jenn wished she were more like Robert, who didn't seem to feel any of that. But she did. She felt all of it, and it was overwhelming. She tried to wear a mask, knowing it was what Robert wanted, especially when they were out in public, but it was hard.

Her ten-year-old son had been one of the last children to be found.

"I'm sorry, Charity. But as far as I'm concerned, you should never have to set foot in that school again."

"I can't believe you. This isn't about you. It's about me going to my school, seeing my friends, and learning to live life again. Unlike you who doesn't want to live at all," Charity mumbled before she ran back up the stairs and slammed her bedroom door.

Jenn winced as the sound echoed through the house.

2

CHARLOTTE STONE

SWEAT DRIPPED down Charlotte's face as she bent over, hands anchored on her knees while she struggled to breathe. She'd killed it today, and it felt good. Great even. She reached for the towel at her feet and wiped her face and neck before standing up straight and stretching. The sounds of the buff fitness instructor on the television screen congratulated her for an excellent workout as Charlotte reached for her water bottle and gulped it down.

She needed that. She'd let her workouts slide in the past few weeks, and it showed. Her patience was thin, her energy low, and she was starting to get fidgety. But after this workout, she felt good. Sore, but good. Energized even. As if she could handle anything that came her way.

She made her way up the stairs, taking two at a time, not ready to let the burn leave her yet, and poured a cup of freshly brewed coffee. She'd bought new beans yesterday and ground some up before heading down for her workout. The aroma of those beans still filled the air, and she knew it would be a good cup of coffee. Exactly what she needed.

She picked up the mail she'd set to the side yesterday and sorted through the abundance of letters that still came in. Letters from various students and families from Stillwater Public School, and even from people who didn't live in their town but had been moved by the tragedy, as if it had touched them personally. All letters Jordan rarely opened, let alone read.

She flipped through all the envelopes and set aside the three addressed to Jordan with childish lettering. She didn't understand his hesitation when it came to opening them. Stacks of similar letters filled a shoe box in her office, so many letters praising Jordan for his heroic acts and describing how his selflessness saved countless lives. She still teared up when she read the ones from the younger students thanking him and calling him their hero.

He was a hero. She knew it. The town knew it. The world knew it. But sadly, she didn't think Jordan realized it.

The sliding door off the kitchen opened, and a cool breeze wafted around her ankles. Charlotte set the letters down and glanced over her shoulder to see her husband standing at the door, his back to her, while he banged his running shoes together to get rid of the sand. His navy running shirt and shorts were drenched and so was their dog, Buster, who plopped down on their back deck with his tongue hanging out.

"Looks like you two had a good run." Charlotte took a sip of the strong coffee before she set her cup down on the counter and poured some for her husband.

"You should come out sometime with us," Jordan offered his obligatory request, same as he did every morning.

"Maybe next time." The words were automatic, but they both knew she'd never join him. Running was his thing. Not hers.

Jordan grabbed his coffee, placed a kiss on her cheek, and

made his way to the guest bathroom where he always showered off.

Charlotte hated to clean a trail of sand throughout the house, so when they built the guest addition to their home a few years ago, she made Jordan start cleaning up in there after his runs.

While he headed downstairs, she went upstairs to their bedroom and had her own shower. Afterward, with her hair still wet, Charlotte took her coffee into her office. She needed to get a head start on today. She planned to go to the public school, where Jordan served as principal, and then spend the day there with the students and any parents unwilling to leave their children alone.

Not that she blamed them. Her hands shook slightly as she sank down in her desk chair and reached for the *Stillwater News*, the weekly paper that was little more than a gossip column for the town. She'd been worried about the front-page article and even asked Arnold Lewery, the editor of the paper, to let her take a peek at what he'd written, but ever since the media had swarmed their town and refused to leave, Arnold had become tight-lipped about what he featured in the paper.

In the beginning, almost every article he wrote, whether it was a piece about one of the families affected by *the event* or a new development, he'd been scooped by one means or another. Their town had become overrun with media within hours of the shooting, and they still couldn't walk down Main Street without a microphone being stuck in their faces or the knowledge they might see themselves on the evening news.

They'd managed to hold a few special town meetings without alerting the media presence, and it became quite evident that everyone, including Arnold, expected her to fix the mess they were in with the media and to shelter them from prying eyes.

"Staying Strong" read the title on the front page. Charlotte was pleased to see the image she'd submitted via e-mail to Arnold last week. She was glad he used it. There'd been too many images of the school ensconced with police tape, memorial flowers, and weeping parents. This photo, taken last year right before the annual summer parade, featured welcome banners, balloons, and children's play centers set up at the school for the summer party. Starting at Stillwater Public, the parade always made its way down Second Bridge, across Main Street, and then up First Bridge until everyone joined together back at the school for the festivities. She hoped the image would help the town remember the good things about Stillwater Bay and not the sad, horrific event that had torn them apart.

She knew not everyone was on board with the school reopening. She'd had more than enough parents complain and demand that the school stay closed, and while she attempted to understand their pain and knew they only spoke out of fear, she had to look past the emotional impact of the school shooting back in May and look to their future.

She was determined that today would be the first of many steps their town needed to take to move forward past the ugliness of what had happened.

Charlotte flipped through the paper, reading the letters to the editor and the small-town gossip, and almost missed the short article written about Julia Berry, the mother of the shooter. She set the paper down on her desk and leaned back in her chair. Her heart went out to Julia. If anything, what had happened was as much Charlotte's fault as anyone else's, including the mother of the sixteen-year-old shooter.

From day one, everyone knew Gabriel Berry had bad blood in him. He was that boy who was always in trouble. The moment he stepped foot into a store, all shop owners knew to keep their gaze on him. She'd lost track of the number of times she learned from the town sheriff's weekly updates that Gabe Berry had been escorted home in the middle of the night after deputies found him hanging around the local cemetery. Who lurked around a graveyard in the middle of the night? It wasn't *natural,* people said.

No matter what anyone did, how they reached out to him, it never seemed to matter.

Since the shooting, Charlotte couldn't shake the feeling that all of them shared responsibility for failing to help Gabriel. The blame couldn't be directed at any one person, no matter how much the media tried to do just that.

She glanced down at the article again: "One Bullet, One Boy and One Mother."

A shiver ran down her spine as she read the lie in that headline over and over and over.

3

JENNIFER

JENN TUGGED the edges of her housecoat tighter as she sat outside on her back deck.

She felt guilty for not taking Charity to school. Not enough for her to change her decision, but enough that she knew she'd handled the situation wrong. Jenn couldn't imagine she was the only parent not okay with the school being opened; no doubt there must be others. What were they doing this morning? Had they argued with their kids as well, or had it been a mutual decision?

It was the beginning of summer. Thanks to the spring rain, the grass was a vibrant green, flowers were blooming, and the trees were full of chirping from the birds nested there. Where had the time gone? Maybe she could talk Charity into helping her with some baking today. They could watch a movie together, eat ice cream, and then meet Robert after work for dinner at Fred's Tavern. No doubt her daughter was up in her room, headphones over her ears as the music blared, anything to pretend her mother wasn't around. She knew this because it's how Charity had acted the past few weeks.

She would either be at her best friend's home or in her room. Anywhere and everywhere, except with her mom.

It hurt, but Jenn was trying to give Charity the space she needed. And, if she were to be completely honest, Jenn hadn't minded the space herself. It meant her life was quiet without any expectations, other than when Robert needed her.

Hiding, withdrawing inside herself, that was how she was coping. If coping was the right word to use.

A lone sailboat sat out in the bay today. Alone, engulfed in silence. Jenn wished she could do that, jump on a boat and set sail, away from all the prying eyes, all the mundane words that meant nothing to her. Alone with her thoughts, with the ability to remain numb without the condemnation from her family and friends.

Life wasn't fair. God was cruel. And yet, none of that mattered. She was still expected to place one foot in front of the other, to move forward with her life, even when all she wanted to do was bury herself in grief beside the son she'd lost.

Robert's voice whispered in her head. *You're still a mother.*

Jenn pushed herself up from her chair and headed back into the house. She refilled her coffee mug, adding an extra shot of Baileys, and noticed that the bottle she had bought only last week was almost empty. She stood there in her kitchen, unsure of which direction to go. Back to bed? Watch a movie? Have a bath?

Or talk to her daughter.

Her feet moved toward the steps as her decision was made. Her counselor had told her to take it one moment at a time.

And in this moment, she needed to be a mother to Charity.

As she slowly climbed the stairs she thought about what she'd say when she opened the door. How would Charity respond? Would she still be upset? She was a thirteen-year-old with mood swings; for all Jenn knew, she could be asleep already.

She knocked on Charity's door and waited. She couldn't hear anything from behind the closed door, so either she had her headphones on or she was asleep. Jenn knocked again, this time louder, but there was still no response. So she opened the door and peered inside.

The room was empty. Charity wasn't in the bathroom either. Jenn ran down the stairs and looked through the house, walking through the rooms, but she was alone. At the front door she realized Charity's running shoes and schoolbag were gone.

Her fists clenched at her side as the sudden onslaught of anger filled her. How dare she!

Jenn grabbed her cell phone and purse, reached for her keys, and called Robert as she made her way to their garage.

"Do you know what she's done?" Jenn said the moment Robert answered his phone.

He sighed on the other end. "I had a feeling she would."

"You had a feeling?" Jenn's words were clipped as she held the phone up to her ear and backed out of her garage. "You had a feeling but didn't bother to say anything to me about it?"

"Why should I? You're the one who is home. I told her not to go to school today, that I'd come home early this afternoon and we could do something together." Robert's voice heated in anger. But she didn't care.

Then his words hit her.

"I'm the one who's home? What do you mean by that? I asked you to stay home this morning." She paused as something down the street caught her attention. "Crap. I can't handle this right now."

"What's wrong?" The Bluetooth function took over, and her husband's voice filled the SUV. Jenn set the phone down and shook her head. She wasn't ready for this. Not yet.

Stillwater Bay was a small town. Nine months of the year the population maxed out at just under three thousand, but in the sum- mer months, from June to the Labor Day weekend, their numbers doubled and sometimes tripled in size, thanks to their proximity to the bay and premium real estate. The landscape on top of the cliffs held million-dollar summer cottages with billion-dollar views.

"The Andersons are here. I don't have their basket made up or anything," Jenn muttered as she drove past their house. There were only five houses on their street, with two facing the bay, one facing the island the town of Stillwater sat on, and two backing onto the golf course. Out of all those houses, Jenn and her family were the only ones who lived there year-round.

"Are they early?"

"Of course they're early." She turned left and headed down First Bridge Street. Two bridges led into their town. The double bridges not only added to the quaintness of their town but also made it special. Ahead of her, in the distance, was her daughter, walking on the sidewalk.

"Found her." The tight band across her chest loosened, and she felt like she could breathe again. Her anger drained as she drove toward Charity.

"You'll take the basket over later, right?"

Robert's words didn't click at first. Baskets. Andersons. Keeping face despite their mourning.

"Of course I'll take over their precious basket. Why wouldn't I?"

"I overheard your talk with Charity the other night regarding the baskets." There was doubt in his voice.

"Then you would have heard my answer." She hoped the exasperation in her voice was loud and clear.

Every word she'd spoken that night to Charity about the baskets was for Robert's benefit. She'd already had this discussion with him and even suggested having someone else do the baskets, someone like his secretary for instance, but he wouldn't hear of it. It wouldn't be the same, he'd argued. People would think we aren't coping, he'd said.

"People expect the baskets. It's a tradition. From our home to theirs. It's a small way to let them know they are wanted in this community, that they matter—"

"It's your way of saving face," Jenn had mumbled. But Robert had heard.

He'd turned to her, placed his hands on her shoulders, and squeezed. "We can either let what happened destroy us or strengthen us." He had then placed a kiss on her forehead and walked away.

The other night she'd been in her office going over her lists, making sure she had enough supplies on hand for these baskets. Charity had stood there, in the doorway, not wanting to come in and help.

"Why do *you* have to do the baskets? Why can't someone else?" Charity muttered as Jenn counted the baskets in her cupboard.

"Like who?" Jenn had responded. "Everyone in this town has been affected by what happened. It wouldn't be fair of me to ask someone else to take on something I love doing." *Or used to love.* She wasn't ready to be social, to put on her happy face.

She drove up close to Charity and, with a push of a button, rolled down the passenger window.

"Need a lift?" The anger she'd felt earlier when she realized Charity had disobeyed her paled thanks to Robert's inquiry regard- ing the baskets. Which was probably a good thing since this really wasn't a battle she needed to fight with her daughter.

"Are you mad?" Charity stepped toward the SUV but didn't open the door. She hefted her schoolbag over her shoulder and looked around.

"More like disappointed. Come on, I'll drop you off."

"I'm sorry," Charity apologized as she got in. She dropped her schoolbag down between her legs and buckled up.

"It's not okay to take off without telling me," Jenn sighed but didn't drive forward. She wanted to have a talk with Charity about this, and the drive to the school would only take two minutes at the most.

Thankfully, her daughter had the decency to look contrite.

"I know. It's just that Amanda and I had plans, and we promised Principal Stone that we would help out with the younger grades."

"I see." Jenn wasn't too happy to hear that last bit. "When did you talk to Principal Stone about this?"

Charity fiddled with her fingers. "Well, I didn't, but Amanda did. I think." She shrugged. "We talked about the idea at least."

"Why didn't you tell me this earlier? When I asked?" "Would it have mattered?"

Silence was Jenn's only reply.

As they made their way over the bridge and passed through the downtown area, Jenn kept her attention focused on the road ahead of her and not on the small crowds of people who lined the side- walks, waving at the vehicles as they passed with banners and signs. "Why are they doing that?" Charity scrunched down in her seat as if to hide herself. Jenn understood the feeling. She noticed Samantha Hill, the lone reporter left from the outside world, in the crowd. For over a month, massive throngs of media had swarmed their town. Once the funerals were held and things quieted down, most of the media had left. All but the one reporter from UCN.

"Mom?"

"I think they just want to offer you guys support."

"That's kind of nice, right?"

Jenn nodded. Sure, it was nice.

"I didn't expect so many people to be here." She glanced over at the school parking lot, on the corner of First Bridge Street and Pelican Street, where the only school in town was located.

"There's Amanda. Can you drop me off here?"

Jenn pulled over to the curb and turned her blinker on. She was thankful she didn't have to drive closer.

"I'm going to hang with Mandy after school, okay?" Charity unhooked her seat belt and opened the passenger door.

"That's fine. Love you," Jenn called out. She wasn't sure if Charity had heard her since she slammed the door, but she did give her a small wave. Jenn watched her daughter link arms with her best friend and walk toward the school together.

That day had started out like any other. She'd made the kids breakfast and they'd rushed to school, running a little late due to Charity having to change her outfit three or four times that morning. On the drive down to school, the kids fought, with Bobby upset about being late and worried that he'd have to get a late slip and stay after school. Jenn had gone in with the kids and signed them in at school; said hello to Jordan, the school principal, as he walked with the kids down the hallway to their class; and waved at the kindergarten teacher, who hustled her kids from the cloakroom into their class. She remembered the sound of her cell phone ringing and the feel of her keys digging into her palm as she searched her purse for the phone. She'd pushed the school doors open with her hip as she answered her phone and bumped into *him*, Gabriel Berry, on her way out.

Those next few seconds were forever etched in her mind. If she'd been paying attention, if she hadn't been on the phone, if she'd actually stopped to think about why that boy—especially that boy—was at the public school and not at his own school, maybe things would have been different.

She pictured Gabriel as they bumped into one another, the scowl on his face, the frantic, wide-eyed look. She should have known; she should have noticed. But instead, she'd been on the phone with her lawyer, who'd called to make sure she'd received the documents.

It wasn't until she'd made her way to the parking lot, almost at her SUV, before she heard the first shot. And then the screams through the open windows.

Jenn covered her ears as the screams replayed in her mind,

over and over and over. For days afterward she thought if she could just concentrate hard enough, she'd be able to pick out the different voices from those screams and maybe, just maybe, hear her son.

Lost in thought, she screamed herself as someone knocked on the passenger door window.

———

THE DOOR OPENED and her best friend, Charlotte Stone, the mayor and wife of Principal Jordan Stone, popped her head in.

"What's wrong? Are you okay?" She held the door open wide and stood there, a look of concern on her face.

"You scared me." Jenn waited for her heartbeat to return to normal while Charlotte opened the door farther and sat down in the passenger seat.

"Sorry." She reached across and grabbed Jenn's hand. "How are you doing?"

Jenn leaned her head back against the headrest and rubbed her forehead. She stared out the open sunroof at the dark-gray clouds as they rolled in and had the sudden desire to drive down to North Beach and view the bay as the turbulent wind rolled in.

"Char, I love you, but would you please stop asking me how I'm doing?" She kept her gaze upward, counting how long it took for the massive cloud to pass over her. "Isn't there something else you could ask that doesn't start with needing to know how my mental state is?"

"Jenn . . ."

"No. Seriously. Can we just agree not to ever ask each other how we're doing? Ever? If I need to talk, trust me that I'll talk, and I'll do the same for you. Okay?" She turned her attention from the clouds to her friend and caught the wariness in her gaze.

"I'm okay. I promise."

"Fake it till you make it," isn't that what they always say? She doubted she'd ever be okay from losing her little boy, but she wasn't the only one in town who had suffered a loss that day. She needed to focus on that.

She could tell from her best friend's gaze that she didn't believe her.

"Do you have time for coffee later? There's something I want to discuss with you."

Jenn's brow rose. All she wanted to do was head back home and bury herself under mounds of covers while the storm rolled in. And maybe make herself a drink.

"I'm not really dressed for coffee." She wasn't in the mood to socialize, even if it was with her best friend.

"Just meet me for coffee at Gina's in about an hour. That should give you enough time to freshen up, right?"

The school bell rang, and Charlotte opened the door. "Please?"

"What are you doing here at the school?"

"Supporting Jordan. He's not as tough as he appears to be. This has shaken him more than I'd like to admit."

"So why open the school even if for a few hours? Why allow our children to relive the horrors? Don't you think they've gone through enough?"

"They need closure. All the psychologists I've spoken to say the same thing." She reached for the door and closed it before sitting back in the seat with a dejected air. "There's not much I can do, but this . . . this I can. Give closure, help others to heal." She pointed toward the school yard. "Besides, you know we closed off all the main areas where . . . only the gym and the front of the school are open, and we have outdoor activities planned for the morning."

Jenn shook her head.

"Not good enough, Charlotte. I'm telling you, as a parent, the worst thing you could have done was open that school, even for half a day. We need to put this behind us, to move on . . . this isn't the closure our kids need."

This wasn't the first time she'd voiced her opinion about this whole issue to her friend. She'd been open about it from the very beginning.

As far as Jenn was concerned, the school should be torn down and a memorial put in its place. Another school could always be built elsewhere.

4

CHARLOTTE

A SWELL of pride filled Charlotte's heart as she watched the parents and children make their way onto the school grounds. She thought for sure more parents would feel the same as Jenn, and if truth be told, she had doubted many would show up today. Never had she been happier to have been proved wrong.

"Hi, Mayor Stone," the cheerful voices of a group of girls called out to her as they passed her. The four girls all had their arms linked together as they headed toward the front doors.

The resiliency of children amazed her. To experience something so horrific, to have their innocence stolen at such an early age and in such a terrifying way and still be able to smile, it stole her heart. It made her to want to be a better person, to look at life differently, to stop looking at the future and enjoy the moment.

Jordan stood at the front door, in his suit, and welcomed each student into the school. Some he shook their hands, others he gave a side hug, but not one student managed to slide past him without a greeting. That's the one thing she loved about him so much, his gentle heart. He had been the perfect principal and the perfect partner and husband during the aftermath of the shooting. The perfect hero to the children in that school.

"Mrs. Stone?" A tiny hand tugged at hers. Charlotte knelt down to face little Ellie Thomlin.

"Hi, Ellie, I love your dress." Charlotte fingered the hem of the pink dress Ellie wore. The material was so soft, and she knew her mother, Lauren, had made the dress herself.

"My mommy made it." Ellie wore a proud smile on her face as she swayed her dress so it billowed out.

"It's beautiful, just like you." Charlotte smiled up at Lauren, who gave her a small nod. Lauren's face was tense despite the smile she gave her daughter. It was the same look on Jenn's face earlier. Lauren's blond hair was pulled back into a tight braid, and she looked like she'd lost some weight, which wasn't a good thing since Lauren was in the middle of battling breast cancer.

"Will you come with me into the school?" Ellie's soft voice whispered.

Charlotte reached her hand out and waited for Ellie to take it. "Of course."

Ellie had been one of the children hidden in a closet on that fateful day. Lauren had mentioned over coffee that Ellie was still afraid of the dark and close spaces. No doubt she always would be. "Are you looking forward to the Teddy Bear Picnic next week?" Charlotte asked as they slowly made their way toward Jordan. She noticed the way Ellie tried to hold back, making her steps smaller and smaller the closer they got to the front doors.

Ellie nodded.

"I think we might need more teddy bears, though, would you like to help me pick some out?" Charlotte glanced over at Lauren as she said this. She knew she should have asked first and hoped she hadn't overstepped.

"Really?" Ellie's eyes brightened.

"If it's okay with your mom," Charlotte added. "Please, please?" Ellie begged.

Lauren swung Ellie's hand, which was clasped tight in hers, and smiled down at her daughter. "Of course."

Charlotte winked at her before she wrinkled her nose at Ellie. "It's a date then. How about I pick you up Sunday after breakfast? We can walk downtown and go through all the stores looking for the best teddy bears they have, okay?"

Ellie gave a deep nod of her head but then stopped dead in her tracks. They'd reached the end of the grass and were only feet away from Jordan and the front doors.

"It's going to be okay." Charlotte stroked Ellie's hair and wanted to cry as her little body trembled. "You're very brave, Ellie."

The little girl shook her head. "No I'm not."

Charlotte caught Jordan's gaze as he waited for them. She squared down in front of Ellie and gently touched her chin. "But you are. You're here and you even dressed up. Do you know what that tells me?" She paused. "That tells me that you are a very strong little girl who is determined to conquer anything that comes her way."

Ellie's lip quivered before she took in a deep breath and looked up toward her mom.

"Today is going to be a good day, Ellie. I promise." Lauren bent down and placed a kiss on the top of her daughter's head. "We get to choose to have a good or bad day, and today is going to be good. I know it."

Ellie took the first step, from grass to pavement, and Charlotte noticed the way Lauren's shoulder relaxed.

"She's been so scared to come back today," Lauren murmured.

Charlotte reached for her hand. "I'm so glad she did, though. I know it must be hard."

"No, you have no idea how hard." She shook off Charlotte's hand and wrapped her arms tight around her body. "Her nightmares came back earlier this week, and last night she hardly slept. Every time she closed her eyes she could hear the screams. I almost didn't bring her."

A moment of guilt filled Charlotte before she shook it off. No, she wasn't going to go there. The psychologist she'd spoken to had confirmed that the children needed closure and that while today would be difficult, for most it would be a step toward facing their nightmare.

"I'm sorry. Is there anything I can do?"

"You've already done it. She'll have something to look forward to this weekend." She squeezed her hand. "Thank you."

"Miss Thomlin, don't you look like a ray of sunshine." Jordan stepped away from the front door and stopped in front of Ellie. "I think Mary is inside waiting for you." He winked at her.

"Mary's here?" Her voice notched in excitement, Ellie let go of Charlotte's hand and turned to her mom.

"Can I go in now? Can I go find Mary?"

"Let's go find her together, okay?" Lauren mouthed *thank you* to Jordan before she left to trail after Ellie.

Charlotte walked beside Jordan as he returned to his station at the front door. Some stragglers still lingered on the front lawn or in the parking lot.

"Are you ready?" she asked him.

Jordan nodded before he stopped and turned to stare out on the grounds. "Last year this front yard was full of parade floats that parents were getting ready, do you remember?"

"Do you think I made the right decision?" Not just for reopening the school for one day, but also for canceling the annual school parade. She pushed it back to coincide with their July Fourth events.

He shrugged. "Change, no matter the reason, is hard. We should have done something, though, anything to help cement today as a good memory."

She laid her hand on his shoulder. "But you did." The back

grounds of the school were covered with obstacle courses, water balloons, and games for the kids to enjoy.

"Will a little bit of fun in the school playground wipe away the nightmares? You can still see it in the kids' eyes." Jordan rubbed his eye and sighed. "I wish there was more I could have done . . ." His voice drifted off.

"You were there, protecting them when you could have lost your own life. You saved children's lives, Jordan. I'm not sure what more you could have done."

A shadow of . . . something, regret maybe, crossed over his features.

"Principal Stone?"

They both turned and faced the school where Pamela Holden, one of the teachers who taught sixth grade, stood holding one of the doors open.

"Could you come inside, please?"

Anyone passing by wouldn't have been concerned by her words, but with one look at her face, both Charlotte and her husband knew something was wrong. Jordan jogged back toward the doors while Charlotte followed.

In the few seconds it took to make it inside, Charlotte imagined all the worst-case scenarios she could think of, but standing in the school foyer, there was nothing to see. In fact, the area was empty.

"What's going on?" Jordan asked.

"It's Molly." Pamela pointed toward the staff lunchroom while she walked ahead. When she entered the room, she stood to the side and waited for Jordan and Charlotte to join her.

"She's hiding in the closet." Pamela kept her voice low.

Jordan headed toward the closet and sank down to rest on his heels. He didn't open the door, instead leaned toward the small opening and spoke quietly to the little girl inside.

Charlotte sat down on one of the chairs in the room and

watched as Jordan attempted to coax the seven-year-old out of the closet.

While Charlotte couldn't hear what was being said, she did sigh in relief as the door slowly opened and a hand reached out. She wondered how many times this scene would play out with other children.

5

JULIA BERRY

A TINY STREAM of sunshine pierced the darkness in her room, illuminating dust particles in the air and tempting her to crawl out of bed and open the curtains. Instead, she burrowed deeper beneath her blankets and turned her face toward the wall where a photo of Gabe sat on her small dresser.

Her son's face shone with happiness and joy as they stood together, on the beach a few years ago. Gabe would have been around thirteen then. That was the beginning of the end.

A thud, clatter, and then another thud had the walls in her room shaking.

Julia burrowed deeper in her covers. She knew what those thuds meant.

Right now, outside her bedroom wall and soon on her front porch, the ground would be covered with broken eggs and smashed glass bottles. On the outside walls of her home, the words *Murderer, Monster,* and even *Slut* or *Whore* would be graffitied across the whitewashed boards of her cottage home she rented.

She expected an eviction notice anytime. Legally, she wasn't sure if they could force her to move, but morally, she probably should. It's what would be best for the town.

She wasn't the murderer. She wasn't the monster. But she had given birth to one. Somehow, somewhere, something had changed within Gabriel. It was her job as his mother to notice this, to see it, and then do whatever needed to be done to help.

But she hadn't done enough. That much was obvious.

Gabe's smile in that photo taunted her. Had he known, back then, what he would become? He had been a smart kid, blowing her away most days with his knowledge, level of understanding, and ability to read people so easily. She often wondered if he'd learned to manipulate those around him as well.

Her heart squeezed tight as she realized what was happening to her. She was slowly starting to see her son in the same way everyone else did. A monster.

With a groan, she flung the tattered cover of her handmade quilt off and slid her legs from beneath its warmth. She couldn't do this. Not again. She needed to force herself up and move, do some- thing. Her home was a mess; she hadn't cleaned it in weeks. Dishes needed to be done, laundry washed, floors swept . . . but the idea of doing all of that exhausted her.

She reached for her long sweater and dragged it across the bed until she wrapped it around her shoulders and slowly stood, her one hand firm on the small bedside table as the room spun. The room always spun nowadays whenever she got out of bed.

She could hear Lacie's voice in her head, scolding her. *You need to eat.*

Every time she ate something, her stomach rebelled. She wasn't sure if it was the drugs her doctor had prescribed or just her body revolting against being healthy. With the way she was losing weight, maybe she carried her own death wish.

With slow steps, she made her way into the kitchen, her slippers shuffling against the hardwood floor, and she blinked at the image of Lacie standing at her messy kitchen counter.

"I hope I didn't wake you." Lacie glanced over her shoulder and smiled.

"What . . ." Julia moistened her cracked lips. "What are you doing here?" She rubbed the back of her neck and wished she'd pulled her oily hair back into a ponytail.

"Sit down before you fall down," Lacie ordered. "I just wanted to make you some fresh coffee and bring you something to eat for breakfast."

"I don't need to be mothered," Julia mumbled but did as she was told.

"Are you sleeping?" Julia shrugged.

"But you're taking the pills, right?" Lacie turned on the coffee machine.

Julia shrugged again. "I am. I just . . . I don't like how they make me feel."

Lacie grabbed a container and brought it over to the table. She opened the lid and set it in front of Julia.

Homemade double-chocolate muffins. Julia breathed in deep and found herself reaching for a muffin.

"How do they make you feel?"

"Numb."

"I would give anything to feel that way. Anything." Lacie's eyes watered before she blinked repeatedly.

Oh God. "I'm sorry. I'm so . . . so sorry." How could she be so selfish?

"Don't. I can't . . . We promised, right?" Julia nodded.

"You are not to blame. If you want to feel . . ." Lacie shook her head. "Then feel. But you have to promise me that it won't destroy you."

"I promise."

"You've lost way too much weight. You haven't been out of

your house in days and"—her nose scrunched up—"you could really use a shower and some clean clothes."

"I didn't ask you to come here." Julia leaned back in her chair and placed her hands in her lap.

"I'm not leaving until you finish that muffin and drink some coffee."

Julia stared at her dirty kitchen floor and couldn't believe she'd let things go like she had. She'd always taken such pride in her clean home, happy that despite its small size, she'd been able to make it feel cozy and clean. Gabe would be embarrassed to see things now.

"How can you"—she hesitated—"how can you get through each day and not feel like giving up?"

Weary lines covered Lacie's face, and for the first time, Julia noticed how tired her friend looked. Maybe she wasn't handling it well either.

"I have my family to think about. What I want to do and what I have to do are two different things."

"I wish I had done something," said Julia. "Seen something. I feel like it's all my fault, and I need to fix it somehow, and yet . . . I can't."

"So that's why you let people egg your house and spray paint horrible words on the siding? Why you let them treat you like garbage?"

Julia didn't say anything. Yes, that was the reason. Because she felt she deserved it. If it helped them feel better, if it helped them to deal with their grief in a small way . . . then she would take whatever they threw at her.

She didn't think she said that out loud, but she must have because Lacie stood up and gave her a hug, holding on tight.

"Here's what I'm learning. Grief demands an answer, and sadly, sometimes there isn't one. But that's not your fault and it doesn't mean that people can take out their anger on you."

Julia didn't know what to say.

"How people are treating you, it's not okay. This isn't how this town should be reacting. You're not at fault." She sat back down in her chair and pushed the container of muffins forward. "I don't blame you, Julia, for what your son did." Her eyes closed as she paused. "I can't let my grief overwhelm me to the point where I don't recognize myself. I can't do that. And neither should you."

Julia watched as Lacie stood up and busied herself with cleaning her kitchen. Julia finished her muffin and then went over and wrapped her arms around her friend, leaning her cheek against Lacie's back. She could feel the sobs shake Lacie's body as she stood there, crying, but there was nothing she could do. No words she could say to take back the fact that Lacie's child was now gone.

How does one go about apologizing for that?

CONTINUE THE READ AND ORDER
Stillwater Rising NOW!

ABOUT THE AUTHOR

Steena Holmes is a self-proclaimed chocoholic, an avid reader and is a *NY Times* and *USA Today* bestselling author with over one million copies of her books sold world wide.

She grew up in a small town in Canada and holds a bachelor's degree in theology. She is the author of thirty titles, including *Finding Emma,* for which she was awarded a National Indie

Excellence Book Award in 2012 and *The Word Game* which won Best Fiction from USA Best Book in 2015.

She currently lives in Calgary with her family but travels as much as she can – which she then blogs about on www.steenatravels.com.

If you would like to stay informed on Steena's new releases, please visit her website and sign up for her newsletter. www.steenaholmes.com

Let's Connect

www.steenaholmes.com
steena@steenaholmes.com

ALSO BY STEENA HOLMES

Stillwater Bay Series

Stillwater Rising

Stillwater Tides

Stillwater Deep

Abby Series:

Saving Abby

Abby's Journey

Standalone Titles

The Word Game

Memory Series

The Memory Child

The Memory Journal

Finding Emma Series:

Finding Emma

Dear Jack

Emma's Secret

Dottie's Memories

Megan's Hope

Halfway Series with Elena Aitken

Halfway to Nowhere

Halfway in Between

Halfway to Christmas

Made in United States
Orlando, FL
28 February 2023